THE MYSTERIOUS MANSION

"Someone's coming! Run!" shrieked Cecily.

Turning, Sara saw that the others were running away from the Lloyd house at full speed.

"Hurry, Sara, do!" gasped Felicity, as she tore down the driveway. "Old Lady Lloyd may not be dead after all!"

Sara leapt from the veranda and raced after her cousins.

"Wait! Wait for me!" Sara called. As she sped over the unkempt lawn, her foot caught in a tangle of wire concealed in the high grass. With a yelp of alarm, Sara landed facedown on the ground.

For a while she lay prone and panting, feeling pain dart like a needle in and out of her knee. Around her, the long grass shifted uneasily in the wind. A twig cracked nearby. She was about to struggle to her feet, when a hand grabbed her by the shoulder.

"Vandal! Guttersnipe!" a voice hissed. "I have you now!"

Looking up, Sara found herself staring straight into the angry face of Old Lady Lloyd.

Song of the Night

Storybook written by

Fiona McHugh

Based on the Sullivan Films Production
"Old Lady Lloyd," adapted from the novels of

Lucy Maud Montgomery

A BANTAM SKYLARK BOOK
NEW YORK · TORONTO · LONDON · SYDNEY · AUCKLAND

Based on the Sullivan Films Production produced by Sullivan Films Inc.
in association with CBC and the Disney Channel with the participation
of Telefilm Canada adapted from Lucy Maud Montgomery's novels.
Teleplay written by Heather Conkie. Copyright © 1989 by Sullivan
Films Distribution, Inc.

This edition contains the complete text
of the original edition.
NOT ONE WORD HAS BEEN OMITTED.

RL 6, 008–012

SONG OF THE NIGHT

A Bantam Skylark Book / published by arrangement with
HarperCollins Publishers Ltd.

PRINTING HISTORY
HarperCollins edition published 1991
Bantam edition / June 1992
ROAD TO AVONLEA is the trademark of Sullivan Films Inc.

Skylark Books is a registered trademark of Bantam Books,
a division of Bantam Doubleday Dell Publishing Group, Inc.
Registered in U.S. Patent and Trademark Office and elsewhere.

ISBN 0-553-48029-4
UK ISBN 0-553-40577-2

Bantam Books are published by Bantam Books, a division of Bantam
Doubleday Dell Publishing Group, Inc. Its trademark, consisting of the
words "Bantam Books" and the portrayal of a rooster, is Registered in
U.S. Patent and Trademark Office and in other countries. Marca
Registrada. Bantam Books, 666 Fifth Avenue, New York, New York 10103.

PRINTED IN THE UNITED STATES OF AMERICA

OPM   0 9 8 7 6 5 4 3 2

Chapter One

Something about the old mansion made Sara pause. Perhaps it was the huge, spiked, iron gates which seemed to bare their teeth at passers-by. Perhaps it was the dark spruces which closed thickly about the silent house, as though guarding a secret. The place seemed full of dead hatreds and heartbreaks. She sensed weeping, tragedy, perhaps even—she shivered—a *curse*.

Sara stopped abruptly by the gates, so abruptly that Felix, trudging behind her with the empty laundry basket, bumped right into her. Losing his balance, he careened backwards into Cecily, sending her sprawling.

"For heaven's sake, Felix King. Just because Mother and Father have left town for the day, don't think you can behave like a hooligan!" chided Felicity, as she hauled Cecily to her feet and dusted her down. Thirteen years old and the eldest of the three King children, Felicity felt it her duty to baby ten year old Cecily, and to bully Felix, who, at eleven, stood somewhat clumsily in the middle.

"I'm not a hoo-gi-lan," retorted Felix, who never could get his words right-way up. "Sara stopped dead, see? All of a sudden. Like someone reached out an' grabbed her."

"That house did," whispered Sara, staring in at the dark building buried amongst the trees. "I declare, that house reached out and laid its icy hand on my heart."

Felicity sighed. "Must you make a drama out of everything, Sara? That's old Miss Lloyd's house. And in case you didn't know, houses don't *have* hands."

But Sara failed to notice Felicity's sarcasm. Her attention was concentrated on the vast, neglected grounds behind the gates. "Tell me about Miss Lloyd—please, Felicity," she begged.

"Why, the Lloyd family practically founded this town. Along with the Kings, of course." When Felicity King rode her family high horse, she sounded uncannily like her Aunt Hetty, a born schoolmarm. "She's rich as a queen. People around here call her 'Old Lady Lloyd', because she's so rich and mean and proud."

"Only bein' rich hasn't done her a peck of good," added Felix. "Pa says no one's ever seen her smile."

"No one's *seen* her, smile or no smile. At least not for ages. Even *I've* got no idea what she looks like," admitted Felicity, who liked to make it her business to know the appearance of everyone in Avonlea. "Why, Sara Stanley! Where in heaven's name do you think you're going?"

For Sara had drifted over to the imposing gates and laid her hand on the latch.

"You can't go in there. That's trespassing."

Sara's gaze remained fixed on the tangled garden behind the gate. "Perhaps poor Miss Lloyd's dead and nobody knows," she answered. "Don't you think we ought to find out?"

Far up the avenue, out of sight of the children, a dark, hooded shape glided from the cover of the whispering spruces. Up the broad, shallow front steps it skimmed, past the stone urns and even stonier lions flanking the entrance, to the massive front door. Stooping, the figure placed a large fish on the sill, then straightened. As it did so, the hood slipped back, revealing the strong, stern face of Peg Bowen.

Now in Avonlea, when the name Peg Bowen comes up, most people drop their voices. For no-one knows for sure just who Peg Bowen is, or where, in the general scheme of things, she stands. Unlike the other residents, Peg refuses to live in a house in summer. Instead she roams the green fields, living off wild berries and sleeping under broad, starry skies. In winter her abode is a small, lopsided cabin deep in the forest, which she shares with six cats, a three-legged dog, a crow, a matronly hen, a stuffed monkey and a small, grinning skull.

Strange stories are whispered about Peg around Avonlea fireplaces at night. Some say she can turn herself into a black cat whenever she pleases. Others lay the blame for a poor harvest or an ailing cow squarely at Peg's door. Still others claim that Peg knows everything, secret or public, that goes on in Avonlea. For all these reasons and more, people fear Peg Bowen and call her the Witch of Avonlea. But whether Peg Bowen is or is not a witch is a question that only those who really know her can answer.

Now Peg pressed her brown face, seamed with a hundred wrinkles, against the front door. "I've brung you a nice fat fish and some herbs fer yer rheumatics," she croaked. "I'll be back tomorrow to pick some firewood. An' don't you go neglectin' those beans I planted, you hear?"

She waited. The house gave nothing back, not even an echo. With a grunt of concern, Peg bent her ear to the letterbox, listening. No sound came from the shadowy interior. Peg frowned. And then she heard it—from deep within the darkness came a harsh, dry cough. That was all. No movement, no answering voice, just a dreary, disembodied cough. It was enough for Peg. Where there's a cough, there's life, she reckoned, nodding her head sagely.

She was about to fade back into the spruces the way she had come, when she stiffened in surprise. Voices! She could hear children's voices approaching the house. Noiselessly, Peg slipped between the swaying trees and waited.

Sara hadn't really meant to trespass. It had been a bright, shiny morning, the sort of morning that makes you feel upstanding and virtuous without having to make any effort at all, when Uncle Alec and Aunt Janet had dropped their three children and Sara off in front of the church.

Sara had spent the previous night with her cousins at King Farm, where they had played all their favorite games and teased and joked until the old house rang with their laughter.

It hadn't always been that way. When Sara first arrived in Avonlea, she had encountered a certain amount of coldness and suspicion. She was a stranger to her cousins then, sent from Montreal by her father, when his business and reputation had collapsed, to the small hamlet of Avonlea on Prince Edward Island. She had survived those first dreadful days and nights. In the large, clannish King family, the isolated twelve year old had gradually discovered a warmth and companionship she had only read about in books. She felt part of a whole now, and the daily give and take of family life delighted her. She even enjoyed Aunt Janet's steady stream of advice. Aunt Janet was so constantly telling her children to do this or not to do the other thing that they had difficulty remembering half her instructions, and after a while gave up trying.

That morning as they had clambered out of the buggy with a basket full of old clothes, Aunt Janet had been at it again.

"Leave those clothes in the mission box and then quick march over to your Aunt Hetty's. She's expecting you," she had ordered, "Cecily dear, please don't forget to make your bed in the morning. I want you all on your best behavior for Hetty. Mind you, go to bed at a decent hour and—"

Fortunately, Uncle Alec had chosen that moment to urge on the buggy. He and Aunt Janet were on their way to Charlottetown, where they were planning to spend the night. Aunt Janet had had to be content with a last reminder. "And no dawdling on the way, mind!"

There had been no thought whatsoever in Sara's mind of dawdling or even dallying as, standing beside her cousins, she had waved goodbye to her aunt and uncle. But that was before they had passed the tall Lloyd gates. That was before Sara had felt something, something very much like a hand, tug at her heart.

Now, as she ran swiftly up the silent driveway, she reflected that Aunt Hetty would probably already have lunch on the table and would be clucking like a broody hen over their unpunctuality. But when Felix had pushed past her through the gate, yelling that they were all 'fraidy-cats, except him, Sara hadn't been able to resist following him. "I am certainly NOT afraid!" she panted, catching up to him, "If there are any dead people in here, I intend to be the first to see them."

At this, Felix seemed to lose some of his daring. "Dead people? Who said anything about d-d-d-dead people?"

"Why, Miss Lloyd may have been dead for

years, stretched out, stiff and cold, without anyone knowing. By the time we find her, she may be nothing but a shriveled skeleton."

Felix faltered. "A s-s-skeleton? S-say, S-S-Sara...?"

But Sara had raced on ahead.

Felix stopped in the middle of the overgrown driveway, feeling fingers of fear poking him all over. For the first time he became aware of the eerie silence. He could hear his own breathing. He would probably hear his heart too, if he were to stop breathing. As it was, he could feel it, pounding away like a drum.

The sun seemed to have retreated suddenly behind a protective cloud. Darkness had sneaked up over the lane, thickening the shadows. Felix's ears prickled. He held his breath. A rustle of branches made him jump and suddenly—oh cripes, oh criminy—there were two black eyes staring into his, and broken yellow teeth snarling and a skinny arm raised to pounce. With a howl of terror Felix turned and scuttled back to the iron gates.

"Peg Bowen! Peg Bowen's in there. I seen her, the Witch of Avonlea. She gave me a look that'd freeze your blood!" he screamed.

From their position of safety outside the gates, Felicity and Cecily observed his mad, cowardly flight. "You never saw Peg Bowen," sneered Felicity. "You're only making it up 'cause you're afraid to go all the way in there."

Felix gulped. He had so seen Peg Bowen. He knew he had. But he knew that if he ran away from the Lloyd place now, Felicity would call him a 'fraidy-cat until the end of time.

Reluctantly he turned and forced himself to walk back towards the house. His knees felt like two large, wobbly jellies. "I did too see her. I did. I did," he muttered.

"Piffle!" replied Felicity. She held the gate open for her little sister. "Come along, Cecily," she said, feeling brave and smug. "Let's go see what Sara's up to."

Chapter Two

By this time Sara, drawn towards the lonely house by a thread woven of dread and curiosity, was standing on the veranda, her nose pressed against a filthy front window. A queer tickly feeling ran down her spine, as her eyes adjusted to the interior gloom.

A huge, high-ceilinged room, looking as if it had been gift-wrapped by an army of diligent spiders, lay before her gaze. Cobwebs hung from the dust-coated chandeliers. They draped themselves over the shrouded furniture. They ran like gray, lacy banners up and down the empty walls and tied themselves with a gossamer flourish around the cold marble fireplace.

Sara's eyes opened wide in amazement. She had expected to feast her eyes on pomp and finery. She had foreseen gleaming brasses, polished wood, rich velvets and a roaring fire. Instead she saw a stripped, joyless, neglected room. Had not Felicity described this house as belonging to a member of one of the founding families of Avonlea, to a lady "as rich as a queen?" She studied the room intently, sensing a story, trying to fathom the strangeness of it all.

Unnoticed by Sara, the other children had taken possession of the grounds. Their fear forgotten, they raced noisily about, exploring and exclaiming. As each minute passed and Peg Bowen failed to swoop down on them, Felix grew steadily more confident. He felt ashamed of his earlier display of cowardice and began to plan how he could blot it out of his memory. If only he could think of some feat, some deed so daring that everyone would forget all about his screams of terror in the driveway! As he stared at a cracked pane in one of the lower windows, an idea slowly took shape in his mind.

Sara was just about to turn away from the window when a movement within the still room arrested her. A long, bony, white hand reached out of nowhere and curled itself around a heavy poker, which leaned against the fireplace. At exactly the same moment a stone exploded through the window nearest Sara, shattering the glass and setting the spiderwebs quivering. It landed directly in front of the fireplace.

Sara just had time to notice that the poker had vanished, before a cry of triumph from Felix wiped everything else from her mind. "A bull's-eye!! Now who's the 'fraidy-cat, Felicity?"

His only answer was a shriek from Cecily. "Oh no! Someone's coming! Run!!!"

Turning, Sara saw that the others were running away from the house at full speed.

"Hurry, Sara, do!!" gasped Felicity, as she tore down the driveway. "Old Lady Lloyd may not be dead after all!"

Sara leapt from the veranda and raced after her cousins as fast as her legs could carry her. They had a good head start on her and were already rounding a curve in the driveway. Soon they would be out of sight.

"Wait! Wait for me!" Sara called. But they had disappeared round the bend. The gravel crunched and skidded under Sara's running feet. She jumped onto the grass for safety, heading for the driveway. As she sped over the unkempt lawn, her foot caught in a tangle of wire concealed in the high grass. There was a ripping sound and then a horrible thud. With a yelp of alarm, Sara landed face down on the ground.

For a while she lay prone and panting, feeling pain dart like a needle in and out of her knee. Perhaps if she kept quiet, whoever was chasing her might give up and return to the house. She shuddered, thinking of the wizened hand grasping the poker.

Around her, the long grass shifted uneasily in the wind which had blown up since morning. The spruce trees huddled closer together. Somehow the bright, shiny new day had lost its gleam. A tiny black spider crept onto Sara's hand, started across, then changed its mind and scuttled back, as a twig cracked nearby. Sara stiffened. Stealthy footsteps rustled through the grass. Had she been spotted? If only her knee didn't ache so, she could jump up and flee. Surely anything would be better than lying with her face pressed into the ground, expecting at any minute to be caught. She was about to struggle to her feet, when a hand grabbed her by the shoulder.

"Vandal! Guttersnipe!" a voice hissed. "I have you now!"

Looking up, Sara found herself staring straight into the angry face of Old Lady Lloyd.

Chapter Three

It was a face which still showed signs of beauty. The eyes were dark and seemed to smolder. The cheekbones were high and fine. The thick white hair was carefully arranged. Her dress, though faded and frayed, was made of the finest silk. But there was nothing soft about the hand clamped around Sara's shoulder. On the contrary, it felt like tempered steel. Holding Sara in its vice-like grip, it dragged her to her feet, shook her once, but thoroughly, and steered her towards the house.

"Please let go. You're hurting me!" she protested.

But Old Lady Lloyd seemed not to hear. Her breath came in short, angry bursts, punctuated by dry coughs. As they reached the house, she paused.

"I do not normally entertain," she panted. "No one has been invited to climb these steps for years. I am the last of the Lloyds." She leaned for support against a silent stone lion. "Perhaps it is just as well. My family, you see, is under a curse."

"A curse?" gasped Sara, feeling her legs turn to water. Had her very first reaction to the Lloyd mansion been right after all? "What kind of curse?"

Miss Lloyd did not answer. She was staring at Sara's injured knee.

"Blood's been spilt. It must be seen to," she muttered. Roughly, she pushed Sara up the steps, then stopped, as though assailed suddenly by memory. "One *could* say my home has been consecrated by human blood," she murmured. Her voice was different, musing. Her eyes searched the flight of steps. "There!" she said, pointing in triumph to a perfectly normal-looking flagstone. "That is the exact spot where Great-Grandfather Lloyd fell and broke his neck. On the very day this house was completed. Made a frightful mess, so they said." She clicked her tongue disapprovingly, her eyes darting around and around, as though seeking an escape into the past.

Again, Sara felt fear brush her heart. With all her might she longed to run away. But her knee throbbed and Miss Lloyd held her fast. Her mind raced. *Concentrate*, she urged herself silently, *plan*. But it was no use. One might as well order a jellyfish to concentrate as ask her terrified, scattered thoughts to pull themselves together and formulate a plan of escape.

Before she could even open her mouth to call for help, she found herself hauled over the threshold and into a gloomy hallway. With a sound like the clap of doomsday thunder, the heavy front door slammed shut behind her.

"Sit there!" Miss Lloyd commanded, pointing a long, white finger so dramatically at a high-backed chair, that it seemed to jump to attention out of the shadows. "You'll be quite comfortable in that chair. It was my uncle's favorite. He died in it from a stroke."

"Oh, dear," croaked Sara, doing her utmost not to sound as terrified as she felt, "that must have been so very difficult for—"

"Nonsense, child. There's nothing difficult about a stroke. Anyone can have one. You don't have to learn how." She pressed Sara into a sitting position. "Now don't move. I shall return presently."

Without another word, she disappeared into the shadows at the back of the hall.

As soon as she had gone, Sara wriggled out of the chair and limped to the front door. The knob refused to turn. Sara almost sobbed in frustration. She tried again, twisting it this way and that, her terrified hands slipping from the cold brass.

A dry coughing along the corridor signaled the return of Miss Lloyd. As quickly as she could, Sara hobbled back to her chair.

In her long, bony fingers Old Lady Lloyd held a bowl of steaming liquid which gave off a peculiar smell. Smoke wafted up from the dish like incense, enveloping the care-worn face and putting Sara in mind of a medieval sorceress.

"Wh-what's that?" she asked, as Miss Lloyd knelt to apply the evil-looking mixture to her knee.

"This," said Miss Lloyd, "is an herbal remedy prepared by Peg Bowen."

"Peg Bowen? Isn't she a w-witch?"

"If she's a witch, I'm the Queen of England," snapped Miss Lloyd. Her fingers worked skillfully, cleansing and dressing the wound.

"The Queen's dead, Miss Lloyd," ventured Sara.

"And so am I," replied Miss Lloyd dryly. "Or at least I shall be, very shortly."

Puzzled, Sara watched the old fingers gently bind a bandage round her knee. Could a person be truly "mean and proud" and still help another, the way Miss Lloyd was doing?

Her thoughts were distracted by a low, creaking noise which seemed to come from the dark passage leading to the kitchen. It sounded like someone scrabbling at the back door.

Miss Lloyd's hand flew to the poker. "Don't you dare move!" she hissed, as Sara struggled to stand up. "I can't abide people popping up and down like jack-in-the-boxes. Now stay where you are. I have my own way of dealing with intruders." Wielding the poker like a sword, she crept towards the sound.

Sara stared after her. What if her cousins were trying to rescue her, were standing at the back door, unaware that Miss Lloyd was about to pounce?

Like a cat stalking her prey, Old Lady Lloyd moved noiselessly towards the tell-tale sound. In one swift movement, she grabbed the bolt, shot it back and flung open the door.

A man stood there, plump and prosperous. Sparse, gray hair curled sleekly around his ears. In one hand he held an envelope, which he had been in the process of stuffing under the sill.

"Cousin Margaret!" he exclaimed, flushing down to his stiff white collar. "How you startled me!"

"Caught you red-handed, Andrew Cameron. Prying into my affairs like the weasel you are! Now get out the way you came!"

Mr. Cameron straightened his shoulders.

"The back gate was open, Cousin Margaret. You know I worry about your well-being. I wanted—"

Miss Lloyd raised the poker. "Out, I said. Out, before I bring the Lloyd curse thundering down about your ears!"

But Mr. Cameron stood his ground. He held the envelope towards her.

"It bothers me to see you living like a pauper, Cousin Margaret. Please. Take this."

Miss Lloyd's face went white with fury.

"I'd rather die than accept charity! From you of all people, Andrew Cameron! However dreadful my situation may be, I still have my pride. Now get out this minute before I knock you into the middle of next week!" Summoning all her strength, she slammed the door and shot home the bolt.

Sara had followed the conversation avidly, forgetting her own dilemma, until the slamming of the door brought home to her the fact that she was a virtual prisoner inside the strange house of an even stranger woman. Taking herself resolutely in hand, she commanded common sense from her scurrying thoughts. One thing seemed plain—she must get away.

Slipping from the chair, she tried the front door again, taking care to turn the handle slowly all the way round. This time it worked. The door creaked open. A gust of fresh air blew into her face, restoring her to reality. Sara stepped gratefully out into the warm, afternoon light.

As fast as her bandaged knee would allow, she limped down the steps, across the gravel and over the grass toward the driveway.

Behind her, she could hear Old Lady Lloyd calling. Without stopping, Sara glanced back. Miss Lloyd stood framed in the doorway, the poker still clenched in her fist.

"Come back!" she called. "I haven't finished with you yet."

But Sara had no intention of going back. Not yet, anyway. She needed time to think about the contradictory Miss Lloyd and the family curse she invoked so freely.

Chapter Four

As the eldest of the King tribe, Hetty King took her responsibilities seriously. She had been horrified when her nieces and nephew had burst like cyclones into her tidy home, screaming that Sara had been taken prisoner by old Miss Lloyd. The idea that any member of the King family might be caught trespassing made her blood run cold. And while they were under her care too! What on earth would Alec and Janet have to say when they returned?

Normally Hetty prided herself on her ability to keep her feelings under tight rein. But the thought of having to face her brother and sister-in-law on their return from Charlottetown made her heart rear up uncomfortably in her narrow chest.

Pausing only to squash her protesting hat onto her head, she had hurried over to the Lloyd place, determined to protect the family's good name at all costs. The three children had scurried after her like a clutch of terrified chickens.

But instead of an outraged Miss Lloyd threatening to haul the entire King family before the courts, Hetty found only her niece Sara, limping towards her down the driveway, looking bedraggled and rather sheepish.

Relieved to see her returned to them in one piece, the other children crowded around Sara, besieging her with questions.

"Say, Sara, that p-person with the poker? W-was she a ghost? Or was it really Miss Lloyd?" Ever since the tall white figure had appeared at the front door, taking them all by surprise, Felix had been in an agony of fear that in breaking the window he might have raised the dead.

"Of course it wasn't a ghost, Felix," snapped Felicity. "Miss Lloyd was dressed entirely in silk. I could tell, even from a distance. Everyone knows ghosts don't go in for silk!"

"What did she do to you, Sara? Did she hurt you?" asked Cecily, slipping her little hand into her cousin's.

"No, she didn't hurt me, Cecily. She took me into her house, which is dark and very dingy. She says it's cursed."

"Thank goodness you came out of there alive!" breathed Cecily, her eyes wide with amazement at Sara's daring.

Hetty's sharp voice cut through the children's welcoming clamor like a saw blade. "Sara Stanley, what in heaven's name possessed you to trespass in Margaret Lloyd's garden?"

"We thought perhaps Miss Lloyd was dead, Aunt Hetty." Sara shivered as the memory of that dust-filled drawing room floated back into her mind. "The whole place seemed so dreadfully still and forgotten. Almost as if someone had cast a spell on it."

"Spell my foot! Margaret Lloyd is no more dead than I am."

"You're quite right, Aunt Hetty. Miss Lloyd is very decidedly NOT dead. In fact, I'm quite sure that if Felix had known how alive she is, he'd never have broken her window."

Aunt Hetty's jaw dropped. "Window? What window?"

Felix glared at Sara. "It was already half-broke anyway," he muttered.

"Felix King, do you mean to stand there, bold as brass, and tell me you broke a window on

Miss Lloyd's property?"

A tremble had appeared in Aunt Hetty's lower jaw. White-faced with fury, she reached out and grabbed hold of her errant nephew's ear. Perhaps Miss Lloyd would have her day in court after all, at the expense of the King family's good name! In her agitation Hetty pulled hard at the offending lobe, her mind filling with the sounds of the judge's gavel and the excited whispers of the gossiping, inquisitive crowd. A squawk of protest from Felix failed to distract her from the events unfolding, as though in a nightmare, before her horrified eyes.

"Ow, that hurts, Aunt Hetty! Let go!"

Perhaps, even now, at this very moment, an angry Miss Lloyd was instructing her solicitors to set in motion the legal wranglings which would besmirch the King reputation, would trample it through the mud. Indignation flooded Aunt Hetty's soul. She waggled the ear in protest. She, Hetty Euphemia King, could not stand idly by and let such a calamity happen. She must uphold the family honor. Yes, she must fight until the last breath left her body, to prevent the slightest dishonor staining the name of King. She must—

A howl of pain from Felix returned Hetty to reality with a bump. "You'll pull it off, Aunt Hetty. Leggo!!!"

Hetty's fingers released the fiery, swollen appendage. Felix backed quickly out of her reach. "Drat it, Aunt Hetty. Miss Lloyd c'n always get another window, if she's a mind to. But there's no way a fellow c'n grow another ear."

Aunt Hetty turned on her heel, remorse over Felix's reddened lobe making her voice sound even snappier than she felt. "Come along home this minute, the lot of you, before I lose my temper completely." Her face, like a thundercloud, she stormed off down the driveway, followed meekly by the three King children.

Sara hung back. Her knee ached and her mind teemed with confused impressions of Miss Lloyd. She wished she hadn't let it slip about the window. She wanted to apologize to Felix. But already he had been shepherded through the heavy front gates by his bristling aunt, who now waited impatiently for her.

"No dawdling, Sara," she called. "You've already missed lunch and you'll be late for dinner at this rate."

As Sara approached the gate, Aunt Hetty suddenly noticed her knee. In her rush to escape from the mansion, the bandage had slipped down about her ankle and the greeny-brown paste applied by Miss Lloyd was clearly visible.

"Dear God in Heaven tonight!" gasped Aunt

Hetty. "What on earth is that revolting concoction all over your knee?"

"It's an herbal remedy, given to Miss Lloyd by Peg Bowen, Aunt Hetty."

Aunt Hetty's cup of fury brimmed over. "Peg Bowen!" she snorted. "Why that crazy vagrant wasn't locked up years ago is beyond mortal understanding!"

So saying, she fairly pushed Sara ahead of her through the gates and slammed them shut. In glum silence the group made its way towards Aunt Hetty's house.

Perhaps, thought Sara, remembering how lighthearted they had all felt earlier that morning, perhaps Miss Lloyd is right and there really *is* a curse after all.

As quietness once more resumed its dominion over the Lloyd estate, a dark figure emerged from the bushes.

"Crazy, is it?" murmured Peg Bowen, a crooked smile surprising her stern face. For a minute she stared after the departing group, her gaze coming to rest on Sara's blonde head. Then she turned back into the tangle of trees. As she walked, a fragment of a time-old proverb turned round and round in her head. "For every evil under the sun," she whispered, "there is a remedy or there's none." She puffed thoughtfully on the old corncob pipe she always carried. "There *is* a remedy. Ay, to be sure," she mused. "And find it we must, afore it's too late."

Chapter Five

By the time the children reached Rose Cottage they were tired and hungry. Lunchtime had long since passed and Felix's stomach was beginning to clamor for dinner.

The old house where Aunt Hetty lived with her younger sister Olivia had been named after the many climbing rose bushes which twined their thorny fingers around windows and doors. Pink, white and yellow roses nodded a welcome from the whitewashed outer walls, their fragrance lending a subtle sweetness to the summer air.

As the family approached the house, a soft, tripping, rippling sound floated from the open windows. Sara stopped and a dreamy light rose in her eyes.

"Why, that sounds just like moonlight would, if it could only speak," she exclaimed. "Did you ever hear such beautiful music, Aunt Hetty?"

Hetty's face expressed a strange mixture of outrage and anguish.

"Dear God. That's piano music. That's what

that is. And it's coming from MY house!"

With a muffled squawk, she hurried into the parlor, where Aunt Olivia sat at the piano, lost in a Chopin sonata. Her nephew Andrew stood beside her, turning the pages.

"Olivia King, have you taken leave of your senses? You know very well I won't allow anyone to lay a finger on Ruth's piano."

Sara always thought of her Aunt Olivia as being just like a pansy—all velvet and purple and gold. Now Aunt Olivia added crimson to her spectrum of colors, as she flushed to the roots of her dark hair. She was many years younger than her sister. Where Hetty planted both feet squarely on the ground, Olivia tended to float away into dreams. Where Hetty was definite, sometimes fierce, Olivia tended towards timidity and mildness.

"I hoped you wouldn't mind, Hetty. It needed to be tuned, so Andrew helped me take the covers off. And then, well, I just couldn't resist playing it a little." Olivia's fingers lingered on the keys. "I really don't think Ruth would have objected."

Puzzled, Sara gazed from her younger to her elder aunt. Both stood stiffly, gazing at each other. Both, for some reason, had tears in their eyes. It came to her suddenly that they were talking about her own mother.

"Do you mean that this...," her fingers barely tipped the ebony lid, "this piano belonged to my... mother?"

"Don't you touch it," snapped Hetty. "Olivia, I want you to cover it up decently, just the way it was. Sara Stanley, did you hear what I said?"

But Sara seemed to have been afflicted with sudden deafness. She moved towards the piano as though attracted by a magnet. Reaching out, she stroked the ivory keys. "My mother," she whispered. "Her hands touched these same keys...."

Felix snorted. "She didn't play 'em with her feet, that's for sure."

"Go wash that muck off your knee this minute, Sara," ordered Hetty. Her voice had an edge of distress to it. "You do as I say, Olivia, and cover it up the way it was."

Normally Olivia dreaded any confrontation with her dogmatic elder sister, but there comes a time when even the most timid of souls must gird for battle. She took a deep breath. "Hetty," she said. "Sylvia Grey will have need of the piano when she visits. That's why I wanted to tune it."

Hetty paused in the act of freeing her crushed hat from its prison atop her head. "Just because a person is musical doesn't mean she can expect *pianos* wherever she goes! I can't allow just anyone to play Ruth's piano, Olivia. You do realize that, don't you?"

"Sylvia isn't just anyone, Hetty. She's a gifted singer, who will require a piano to practice on. Besides, it will help her feel at home. The poor soul has no one left in the world to care for her."

"Please, Aunt Hetty, I don't know who Sylvia is," chimed in Sara. "But I can't help feeling for her, if she's all alone in the world. A piano might ease her heart. As for me, if you cover it up, it would be just as if mother died all over again."

"I am sick to death of you and your theatrics, Sara. You children seem to have death on the brain. One more peep out of any of you and it's bed with no supper."

Felix rose instantly to a perceived challenge. "Peep?" he ventured in a mischievous whisper. "Peep, peep, peepity-peep!"

Something in Hetty snapped. "That's it. That's the very last straw. Off to bed with you this minute, Felix King."

Felix's smile faded. He looked around, hoping his Aunt Olivia would defend him. But Olivia was staring at Sara, who had flung both arms along the piano keys in an impulsive gesture of protection.

"I'm sure Ruth would have wanted others to enjoy her piano, Hetty," said Olivia gently.

"Especially her only daughter."

A single tear crept down Hetty's cheek and plopped onto the hat she now held in her bony hands. She blinked. "Ruth loved that piano so..."

Sara lifted her face from the keys. "Please, Aunt Hetty. Hearing mother's piano would make me feel as if a tiny part of her were still alive."

Hetty swallowed. Her voice sounded hoarse. "Very well, if you all insist." She turned away, striving to control her emotions. It was years now since her favorite sister, Ruth, had died. At the time Hetty had attempted to bury her grief under a multitude of domestic and community activities. Ruth's beloved piano had been pushed back into a corner of the parlor, where it had stood, covered and silent, through summer and winter. As the years passed, its flattened top had been used to display framed family portraits and silver knickknacks, until its original musical purpose had been all but forgotten.

Now, unexpectedly, its voice had sung out, stirring memories in Hetty, which threatened to bring her grief flooding back.

Sensing her aunt's distress, Sara crept up to her, putting her arms round her waist. "Thank you, Aunt Hetty. Thank you, thank you, thank you," she whispered.

Aunt Hetty patted her head, unable to speak.

Then, shaking herself all over, as if she could shake off her grief, she began bustling about the kitchen. All Avonlea, it seemed, would come to a standstill, were dinner not to appear on the King table within the hour.

It occurred to Felix, watching his aunt out of the corner of his eye, that she might, in her preoccupation, forget all about her ridiculous bed-with-no-dinner scheme. Whistling quietly under his breath, he began to sidle towards the back door and freedom.

Hetty's voice brought him up short. "I meant what I said, Felix. Up to your bed at once."

"Must I go at once, Aunt Hetty? I'm feelin' awful hungry, seein' as how I missed lunch an' all."

In reply Aunt Hetty took him by the elbow and propelled him to the stairs.

"Couldn't I have some grub first? Just a crust, Aunt Hetty, please."

"Not one single bite. Now up to bed with you, before I chase you there with the broom."

"I'll eat twice as much for breakfast," threatened Felix. But Hetty had already dismissed him from her thoughts and returned to the kitchen. Felix turned on Sara, hunger and fatigue lending cruelty to his tongue.

"You had to go an' squeal about the window,

didn't you? Gettin' her wound up tight as a spring."

"I didn't mean to. It just slipped out."

"Squealing like a little piggy, that's all you ever do. I wish you'd never come to King Farm. I'm sick of listenin' to you and your silly stories."

"Well YOU never, ever say anything worth listening to, Felix King. Not once. Not even by accident!"

"You think you're so all-fired smart, don't you? Well let me tell you I'm glad your mother's not here any more. I'm glad I don't have to listen to the both of you thumpin' on that foolish old piano. I'm only sorry you came here in the first place. No one wanted you to come. You know why? Because your father's an emburglar, that's why!"

Sara stared at Felix in disbelief. Tears pricked at the back of her eyes but she refused to let them come.

"You are a low, despicable creature, Felix King, and I'll never forgive you. NEVER!"

Turning, she fled the room.

Andrew got up from his seat by the fireplace and walked over to Felix, who eyed him warily. Although Andrew had not lived in Avonlea long, there was something about this quiet, self-contained fourteen year old, which made Felix anxious to win his respect.

Andrew had arrived on Prince Edward Island at the same time as Sara. His father, Alan King, a widely-traveled geologist, had been sent to South America by his company, and had arranged for his only son to stay with his cousins on the King homestead while he was away. Of all the children, Andrew probably had the most in common with Sara. He was as accustomed as she to a solitary life. He had lost his mother just as she had, although Andrew had been older when his mother died, and thus remembered her more clearly. Seven years had elapsed since then, but still he missed his mother's presence. The idea that Felix could taunt Sara with her mother's absence and her father's financial difficulties shocked him deeply. He stared down at his younger cousin, his face stern. "What's gotten into you, Felix King? How would you feel if someone were to talk like that about YOUR parents?"

Felix knew how he would feel. He would feel as miserable and hurt as Sara had looked. But it was too late. He had said those mean things and there was no un-saying them. Heaving a sigh, he plodded heavily up the stairs to bed.

Behind the King family orchard, concealed in a hollow between two green hills, lay a pond hedged about with willows and shivering aspens. Ever since her arrival in Avonlea, Sara had felt a kinship with this small expanse of sparkling water. She loved to hear the frogs singing from the stones and watch the buttercups flicker like tiny lights amidst the grass.

Andrew found her there, the tears still glistening on her cheeks.

"Won't you come in for dinner, Sara?" he asked quietly.

"I can't possibly grapple with dinner right now. I feel much too discouraged and sick at heart."

Andrew sat down on the grass beside her. "He didn't mean it, Sara. Felix never thinks before he speaks."

"He did mean it, every word."

Andrew fell silent, wondering how to comfort his strange, story-telling cousin, of whom he had grown immensely fond in the short time he had known her.

Sara had been sent from Montreal to live with her cousins after her father had been charged with embezzlement. Before she left, he managed to explain to his terrified daughter that an unprincipled business associate was responsible for his firm's financial collapse, and that he himself was innocent of all wrong-doing.

But the scandal had spread even to the sheltered community of Avonlea. Sara's loyal heart was constantly pierced by sneering remarks about her father. To hear Felix, her own cousin, repeat such allegations confused and frightened her.

Andrew put his arm around her shoulder. "You're not alone, you know. I believe in his innocence too."

Taking a handkerchief from her pinafore, Sara dried her tears. "Thank you for that," she whispered.

Andrew jumped to his feet. "Now come along, before Hetty thinks your knee's affected your appetite."

"Please inform Aunt Hetty that I shall be in shortly—just as soon as I make up my mind how to wreak vengeance on Felix King."

There was a determined tilt to Sara's chin and a gleam in her eye, which made Andrew glad not to be in Felix's shoes.

Chapter Six

The next day, everyone at Rose Cottage rose up with the lark, for it was the morning of Sylvia Grey's arrival. Aunt Olivia whisked about, cleaning and polishing, her face wreathed in smiles, until Aunt Hetty finally snatched the feather duster from her in exasperation. "For mercy's sake, Olivia, the house is neat as wax. Would you stop fussing and put your hat on, or Miss Grey will think you've forgotten to fetch her."

"Dear me, I do believe you're right, Hetty. Just look at the time. Hurry children. Into the buggy or we'll be late!"

In honor of Olivia's guest, Felicity and Cecily were wearing their new summer muslins. They climbed into the back of the buggy, taking care not to crush their finery. Felix had no such qualms and jumped aboard so clumsily that he fell on the floor, causing a cloud of fine dust to rise around the girls. Felicity hardly noticed, such was her excitement at the thought of meeting a singer. "I've never met a truly gifted singer before, Aunt Olivia. Should I curtsy to her, I wonder?"

"Is Sylvia famous, Aunt Olivia?" asked Cecily.

"She will be one day," answered Olivia, flapping at the dusty air with her gloves, "if she ever gets the kind of opportunity she deserves. Now where on earth has Sara got to? Andrew, be a dear and see if you can find her."

Before Andrew could descend from his seat

beside Olivia, Sara appeared at the cottage door, wearing a white dress trimmed with French lace, and a charming white hat.

She had been strangely silent all morning and now, as she slowly approached the buggy, there was something regal, almost haughty about her bearing, which made everyone turn in her direction.

"Do hurry, Sara. Sylvia must have arrived by now," pleaded Olivia.

Sara narrowed her eyes and glared up at Felix, who was slumped in his seat. "I'm not setting foot in that buggy unless a certain person gets off."

Aunt Olivia stared down at her, taken aback. "Why, Sara! Whatever do you mean?"

"I mean either Felix goes or I go. I refuse to share the same carriage with a pig."

"You mustn't talk to your cousin like that!" exclaimed Aunt Olivia in true distress.

"Don't make him get off, Sara," begged Felicity.

"No, please don't," chimed in Cecily, "especially not now that he wants to make up. You do want to make up with Sara, don't you, Felix?"

Embarrassment made Felix cringe. He sank even lower in his seat.

Cecily nudged him. "Go on. Tell Sara what

you told me last night," she whispered.

Felix opened his mouth. All eyes were fixed on him. A rush of shame and awkwardness swept over him. The words of apology he had planned so carefully, stuck in his throat, emerging only as a hoarse mumble.

"You see," flashed Sara, in a tone of cold contempt. "What else can you expect from a pig but a grunt."

Felix clambered to his feet. His face burned as though it had been slapped. "I'm not gonna stay where I'm not wanted. You can all go without me. I'm not too pertic'lar 'bout meetin' no high an' mighty singin' lady anyhow."

Jumping out of the buggy, he stalked into the house without a backward glance. Sara took his place, her head high.

Olivia started the buggy, then turned to her niece with a vexed look. "What a way to behave, Sara. Cousins should be as close to one another as brothers and sisters."

Sara raised her chin even higher. "I have neither brother nor sister to be close to, Aunt Olivia," she replied, "and I refuse to consort with a pig, even if he is a cousin."

The rest of the journey proceeded in silence.

Olivia had met Sylvia Grey while both were

attending the Prince of Wales College in Charlottetown. In keeping with the old adage about opposites attracting, the quiet, dreamy Olivia had struck up an instant friendship with the light-hearted, outgoing Sylvia. Their year in Charlottetown over, Sylvia had gone on to study music in Ontario, while Olivia had returned home to Avonlea. But the bond formed between them had remained strong. Never a week passed without one writing to the other. From the quiet byways of Avonlea, Olivia had observed, with keen and selfless interest, the progress of her talented friend.

When Sylvia had written from Ontario to say that she would be visiting acquaintances in Charlottetown, Olivia had immediately issued an invitation to Rose Cottage, over Hetty's loud objections. Hetty was convinced that a woman who dreamed of a career as a concert singer could hardly fail to exercise a pernicious influence on her unworldly younger sister. To the middle-aged Hetty, who had never been outside Prince Edward Island, Sylvia's willingness to travel from one province to another seemed certain proof of a lack of moral fiber. "You know I don't hold with traveling, Olivia," Hetty had complained. "The way girls roam over the earth nowadays is something terrible."

But Olivia wasn't a King for nothing. Despite her tentative manner, she could be just as stubborn as Hetty. Quietly but firmly she had worn down her elder sister's resistance. She had sealed and mailed the invitation; and then she had waited in mute suspense for the reply.

Sylvia had written back, a warm, grateful letter of acceptance. Her acquaintances in Charlottetown, she wrote, had arranged transport for her as far as the village of Avonlea. She would wait for Olivia at the Avonlea General Store.

Hetty had been obliged to concede defeat, and had watched with ill-disguised resentment, Olivia's growing excitement as Sylvia's visit drew closer.

Now, finally, the longed-for day had arrived. Even the unpleasantness between Sara and Felix failed to dampen Olivia's high spirits. She was on her way at last to welcome her dearest friend to Avonlea. Happiness radiated from her, shedding its warmth so generously that even Sara's icy mood cracked and began to thaw. By the time the buggy pulled up in front of the General Store, merriment was the order of the day. Leaving Andrew in charge of the horse, the others crowded inside.

A tall, slender figure hurried towards them as they entered. Under a straw hat of the most elegant shape and trim were piled masses of wavy chestnut hair. Her dress and coat were of the palest beige, a color which brought out the ruddy gloss of her hair and the clear brilliance of her skin. This vision of loveliness greeted Olivia with frank delight.

"Olivia, my dear. How wonderful to see you again! Why I do believe you haven't changed a bit. When everyone else is a hundred, you'll still look eighteen."

Olivia laughed as she hugged her friend. "And you're as elegant and attractive as ever." Taking Sylvia's hand she drew her towards the three girls, who looked as though they had been struck dumb with admiration.

Despite her new muslin, Felicity felt dull and countrified in the presence of this glamorous stranger, while Sara recognized in the simple straw hat the indefinable, unmistakable flavor of Paris.

Felicity and Cecily both curtsied when they were introduced, without even being aware of what they were doing. Sara shook Sylvia's hand solemnly. "How do you do, Miss Grey," she said. "I can tell by your hat that you are extremely talented."

"Why thank you, Sara," laughed Sylvia, feeling instantly drawn to this serious child with the enormous eyes, "I shall do my best to live up to its pretensions."

As the girls competed with each other to carry Sylvia's luggage out to the buggy, she whispered to them playfully, "First impressions are so important, don't you think? And since I've determined to make a favorable impression on your Aunt Hetty, I felt it of vital importance to be appropriately hatted."

Olivia smiled. "Don't be taken in, girls, she's not half as silly as she likes to appear."

Olivia's merry laugh rang out through the store. "Why, of course I am," she contradicted gaily. "What's the point of being young, if one can't be silly?"

A fragrant wind, bearing with it the scent of spruces, greeted them as they emerged from the store. Sylvia stopped and inhaled gratefully. "The air here positively sparkles! It's as clear and crisp as champagne."

Andrew raised his cap on being introduced. Under Sylvia's candid scrutiny, he felt himself blush.

"How do you do, Andrew?" she said, giving his hand a cordial shake. "I see you have the classic King nose. I'm awfully fond of nice noses. Mine is decidedly un-classic and peasant-like, I'm afraid. But then, we all have our crosses to bear.

You must just accept me as I am, with all my faults, as the Lord made me."

Andrew looked as if he were perfectly prepared to accept Sylvia Grey no matter what her faults. With a huge smile, he took her luggage from the struggling girls and stowed it effortlessly away.

They were all about to climb into the buggy, when Olivia turned to her friend. "It's such a glorious day, Sylvia. Why don't we stroll home through the woods? Andrew will drive the luggage home, won't you Andrew?"

Andrew nodded eagerly. He seemed prepared to drive to the Cannibal Islands and back, if only to please the beauteous Miss Grey.

"Come along, Sylvia. We can wander through all the delightful old haunts I described to you so many times in my letters."

Sylvia slipped her arm through Olivia's. "What a charming idea! And we'll be carefree and giddy as girls again."

She turned towards Felicity, Cecily and Sara who hesitated by the buggy, unsure whether they were included in such an attractive invitation. "Come along, children, do. I'm longing to see *your* favorite haunts as well."

The girls needed no second bidding. They ran towards her gladly, vying to take her hand.

Sylvia's eyes danced. "Just think," she said, taking another deep breath. "Think of the marvelous benefit to the lungs of air such as this. Now, who's for a song?"

Joining hands, the five of them set out along the path towards the woods.

Chapter Seven

Old Lady Lloyd placed a small bunch of wild flowers on her father's grave. She sighed deeply, looking around at the small family plot which lay to the back of her estate, separated from the surrounding spruce woods by a low stone wall. All her family was buried here. She was the last of the Lloyds and she was lonely, lonely, lonely. Weeks would go by at a time without her ever setting eyes on any human being, except Peg Bowen. And Lord knows, she mused wryly, there was some question as to just how human Peg was.

As if sensing the direction of the old lady's thoughts, Peg spoke up from the dark corner of the cemetery, where she was collecting kindling. "I'm near done. There'll be enough firewood here to last the week."

The old lady nodded gratefully. Peg was good

to her. There was no question about that.

The Avonlea gossip which said that Old Lady Lloyd was rich, mean and proud was, as is usual with gossip, one-third right and two-thirds wrong.

Old Lady Lloyd was neither rich nor mean. Once upon a time she had been wealthy, but today she was pitifully poor. She *was* very proud, however, so proud that she would have died rather than let the people of Avonlea, among whom she had paraded in her youth, suspect how poor she was now.

Peg was the only one who knew her secret. Somehow it was all right for Peg to know. Proud as she was, she could accept the small kindnesses of Peg. Perhaps, she reasoned, it was because she now had more in common with an alleged witch than with ordinary folk. She and Peg were both oddities, both outcasts. Poverty had made Old Lady Lloyd an outcast—poverty and pride.

Stooping, the old lady touched the cold granite of her father's gravestone. She had loved him dearly. An upright, honorable man, he had been known throughout the Island for his kindliness and generosity.

"There never was a finer gentleman than old Doctor Lloyd," she had overheard a mourner claim at her father's funeral. "Real generous and neighborly, he was. Always doing kindnesses to everybody, and he had a way of doing them that made you feel as if you were doing the favor, not him."

She sighed again as she rose from the grave and gazed about her. Yes, he had been a kind, trusting man—too trusting perhaps.

The spruce woods around the Lloyd place were all sprinkled through with mellow lights and shadows. But they failed to ease the old lady's distress. Once upon a time she had loved nature, but now it seemed to hurt her. Everything hurt her—the fairy mists down in the little beech hollow below the house, the fresh smell of the red earth, warmed by the sun. It hurt her to remember that long ago she had reached out her hands joyfully to each new day, as though to a friend bringing good tidings. It hurt her to recall how very fond she had been in her early life of company and conversation. There were times when she would have sacrificed everything but her pride for a little human companionship. Old Lady Lloyd had nothing to love, and that is about as unwholesome a condition as is possible for anyone.

The noon sun fell warmly on the old stone wall bordering the graveyard. Miss Lloyd leaned against it, lost in a reverie of times past.

Through the nearby woods meandered a mossy path which, skirting the Lloyd estate, ran up towards King Farm, coming out just above the orchard. Voices and laughter sounded from this path, although to whom the voices belonged, Miss Lloyd could not tell, as the owners were still obscured by close-knit spruces. Leaning over the wall, she scrutinized the forest, then shrank quickly back behind the wall. Through cracks in the sun-warmed stone she could see a group coming gaily towards her down the path. Two young women in front, three children behind them, clinging to the hands of one of the young women—a tall, slim girl.

Starved as she was for companionship, Miss Lloyd could not help but gaze curiously upon these laughing passers-by. And then, all at once, her heart gave a great bound and began to beat as it had not beaten for countless years. Her breath came quickly and she trembled like an aspen leaf. Who—*who* could this girl be?

Thick, copper-colored hair gleamed from under a becoming straw hat, hair of the very shade and wave that the old lady remembered on another head in vanished years. Large, laughing brown eyes flashed from under the straw brim, eyes which the old lady knew as well as she knew her own.

The girl's face, with its glad, buoyant youth, was a face from the old lady's past—a perfect resemblance in every respect save one. The face which Miss Lloyd remembered had been weak, for all its charm. But this girl's face possessed a fine, dominant strength.

As she stopped in front of the old lady's hiding place, the girl laughed in delight at something which claimed her attention from the forest floor. Miss Lloyd knew that laughter well. She had heard it before at that very spot in the woods.

Sylvia was pointing to a patch of woodland, starred over with pink and white flowers. "Mayflowers!" she exclaimed. "My father always described Avonlea as being all a-glimmer with mayflowers, and here they are!"

Olivia looked puzzled. "This is the only spot they seem to thrive. How strange that he should have known about it. I wasn't even aware your father had been to Avonlea, Sylvia."

"He taught school here for one whole term. More than forty years ago," Sylvia replied. "He always said it was the happiest time of his life."

The group moved on up the path towards the farm, their voices fading in the distance.

Old Lady Lloyd watched them until they disappeared over the wooded hill, and then she shook herself as if waking from a dream.

Peg watched her with narrowed eyes. "I seen the way you looked at that girl," she muttered, coming up behind the old lady. "Know her, do you?"

Miss Lloyd's eyes were still fixed on the empty path. "She...reminded me of...of...someone. Someone I knew... a long time ago."

Chapter Eight

From the barn Felix watched the little group moving slowly towards Rose Cottage. Making up his mind, he ran towards the trellis, which framed the front path. With clumsy fingers, he picked a single red rose. He knew Sara's weakness for flowers. He would present it to her and she would recognize it for what it was—a peace offering.

Hiding the rose behind his back, he waited as they came up the path, Olivia in the lead with her laughing friend.

"There you are, Felix," she called. "Come and be introduced to Miss Grey. She's dying to meet you."

Felix found himself gazing up into a pair of merry brown eyes. "How do you do, Miss Grey," he mumbled, extending his hand. Instead of shaking it, Miss Grey merely stared in surprise.

In his confusion, Felix had forgotten all about the rose. It lay there in his outstretched hand like a bright red exclamation point.

"Why, what a beautiful rose!" exclaimed Miss Grey. "And what a gallant young man. It *is* for me, isn't it?"

Felix's face was the color of the rose. He mumbled something which sounded like "yes" and "no" together.

Smiling her thanks, Sylvia fastened the rose to her blouse, then allowed Olivia to draw her towards the house.

Defeated, Felix retreated down the path towards Sara, who had observed the whole scene.

"I meant that rose for you, Sara," he burst out. "I'm sorry I hurt your feelings. It's just that I was awful hungry. It's real hard on a fellow bein' sent to bed with no supper, 'specially when he's hungry enough to eat a horse."

But Sara had closed her heart to Felix. She stared at him with eyes devoid of sympathy.

"Anyone who takes refuge in his stomach," she answered cuttingly, "just isn't worth talking to."

Turning on her heel, she marched away from him.

Evening was falling over Avonlea. In a stream of rosy gold the sun was setting. A drowsy hush had settled on bird and insect alike. The only sound to pierce the twilight peace came from the newly tuned piano, at which Olivia sat, playing softly.

Behind her, Sylvia stood by the open windows. Thinking herself unobserved, she unconsciously relaxed her defenses. Lines of worry crept along her smooth forehead, wrinkling it, and a secret fear clouded her eyes. She leaned out into the dusk with a sigh.

But if Sylvia thought she could hide her innermost feelings from her best friend, she was gravely mistaken. A year of closeness at college and many years of faithful correspondence had taught Olivia much about the vagaries of her friend's moods and the hidden difficulties in her life. She stopped playing abruptly and turned. "I know something's wrong, Sylvia," she said. "Tell me what it is."

The wrinkles vanished. The eyes brightened. The smile reappeared. "Why, nothing. There's nothing wrong."

"Sylvia Grey," said Olivia firmly. "Something *is* wrong and if you don't tell me what it is this minute, I shall shake you."

"Oh, Olivia!" wailed her friend, relief at being

forced to confess making her instantly weepy. "I was born a seesaw, and nothing can prevent me from teetering. One minute I'm soaring skywards in a great burst of happiness. And the next I'm plunged into the depths of despair, convinced I'm about to make the worst decision of my life."

"What kind of decision, Sylvia? What are you talking about?"

"I've been offered a job—a good, sensible job, as a good, sensible music teacher. I should feel happy about it, but I can't, Olivia. I simply can't. Ever since I was a little girl, I've wanted to sing. "

Olivia nodded. She knew all about Sylvia's dreams of becoming a concert singer.

"When Father died, there was just enough money left for me to study music at the Conservatory in Toronto. That's all spent now. I need to go abroad to complete my training, but there's no money left. So here I am, torn between chasing a dream and facing the reality of supporting myself for the rest of my life."

"But you've had so much experience, Sylvia. You've sung at all sorts of events. Audiences have always loved you."

"Yes, but none of them ever paid to hear me. I've always done it for charity up to now. Besides, who knows if I even have the talent to become a concert singer?"

"Of course you do," replied Olivia staunchly. "You must have more confidence in yourself, Sylvia. In future, just remember that little man in Carmody I wrote you about, the one with the terrible lisp."

"I don't think I remember him," murmured Sylvia, wondering what a little lisping man in Carmody had to do with her problems.

"He had a wonderful motto. He would stand up at prayer meetings and remind us all how important confidence was." Olivia did her best to imitate the lisp. " 'Why thine like a candlethick,' he'd roar at the top of his voice, 'When you can thine like an electric thtar?' "

For the moment Sylvia's worries dissolved in laughter.

"How well you know me, Olivia! I'd far rather 'thine like an electric thtar' than be a country schoolmarm for the rest of my life. I'm just not cut out for good, sensible work. I can't help feeling that those whom the gods wish to punish, they first make country schoolmarms!"

"Hush," Olivia said with a grin. "You mustn't let Hetty hear you say such a thing. She prides herself on being the best country schoolmarm for miles around."

"I'm sure Hetty shines in her own, very particular way," acknowledged Sylvia, generosity returning with her good humor.

Sensing the improvement in her friend's mood, Olivia turned back to the piano and continued playing. Sooner or later they would have to find an answer to Sylvia's dilemma. But for now she thought it best to soothe her distress with song.

Sara was pinning the washing up to dry from a line strung across the back veranda, when she heard footsteps approaching the house. She peered through the gray and gold of the fading twilight. A faint, blue-white mist rose from the orchard. In the theater of sky above Rose Cottage, a silver half-moon waited to make its appearance. Sara could discern no human presence. She listened, straining her ears.

Sylvia's clear, rich soprano wafted through the open windows of the parlor.

Alas my love, you do me wrong,
To cast me off discourteously...

Entranced, Sara leaned her arms against the veranda and listened to the song, written hundreds of years ago—melancholy and moving to her, there in the Avonlea dusk, as it was to its first listeners in sixteenth-century England.

And I have loved you so long,
Delighting in your constancy.

The white sheets Sara had pinned up moments

ago blew gently in the breeze, rippling against her, obscuring her from sight. Footsteps sounded again. Peering out from behind the sheets, Sara was astonished to see Old Lady Lloyd moving quietly towards the house. Somewhere between the time Sara had last seen her and now, she seemed to have shed ten years at least. She walked erect and tall, her head high. In her arms a large bunch of mayflowers glowed in the half-light.

As Sara watched, Miss Lloyd laid the mayflowers by the half-open door. Then she stood still, her attention caught and held by the silvery voice.

Greensleeves was all my joy
Greensleeves was my delight...

Sylvia's song seemed to lighten the growing darkness. It radiated from the window—warm, powerful, sweet, and true. Miss Lloyd listened with rapt attention, an expression on her face that puzzled Sara. For she seemed to be listening in the past and in the present at once. She seemed, Sara thought, to *remember* the singer as well as the song.

The song ended. The voice was still. The old lady seemed to drag herself back from her memories.

"Miss Lloyd?" called Sara.

Startled, Old Lady Lloyd turned. Her eyes fell

on Sara standing in the shadows on the veranda.

"Wait, Miss Lloyd, please!"

Miss Lloyd turned quickly away. Sara dashed down the back steps, her progress hampered by billowing sheets. She reached the door. But it was too late. Miss Lloyd had disappeared. On the spot where she had stood lay a bunch of white and pink mayflowers. Sara picked them up. A note was thrust through a stem.

For Sylvia, it read.

Raising her eyes from the note, Sara met the puzzled stares of Olivia and Sylvia, who had just emerged onto the terrace for a breath of fresh air.

"Mayflowers!" breathed Sylvia, catching sight of the bouquet in Sara's arms.

"They're for you. The note says so."

Sara handed the flowers to Sylvia, who buried her face in their fragrant blossoms. "For me! Can they really be for me? Who could have left them here?"

Olivia smiled. "Who knows? You must have an admirer in Avonlea. Do you recognize the writing?"

Sylvia shook her head, her eyes puzzled. She looked around, as though searching for the giver. At that moment, Felix emerged from the barn, where he had been attending to the animals before setting out for home. Sylvia's face cleared.

"Felix King," she called. "What a dear, sweet boy you are. Someone must have told you I have a special fondness for mayflowers. I shall wear some in my hair to church on Sunday."

Felix stopped dead, his mouth falling open in surprise. He started to speak, but Sylvia had already turned back into the house in search of a vase.

Uneasily, Felix shifted his glance in Sara's direction. She was staring at him, a hard, suspicious look on her face. "You didn't leave those flowers." It was more of a statement than a question.

"I never said I did. Anyway, what's it to you?"

"Mind your own business, and I'll mind mine" she replied rudely, lifting her nose high in disdain.

"Better mind it don't rain. You keep your nose stuck up in the air like that, you might drown."

Felix smirked as he stalked home. He couldn't help feeling that for once he had had the last word on Sara Stanley.

Chapter Nine

That night, the memory of Old Lady Lloyd's face, as she listened to Sylvia's song in the gathering dusk, haunted Sara's sleep. When she awoke it was still dark. Rising, she went to her window and raised it slightly. A cool breeze, heralding dawn, wafted in. The slender, crescent moon still graced the night sky, but the stars were beginning to fade. Leaving the window open, Sara climbed back into bed and gave herself over to thought.

Several things had become clear to her. The first was that, despite all the old lady's gloom-filled sayings and practices, Miss Lloyd appealed to Sara. Something about her, she could not yet say what, fired her imagination.

The second was that some connection tied Margaret Lloyd to Sylvia, although Sylvia herself appeared unaware of the old lady's existence. The mayflowers were the most potent proof of this connection. But a conversation, accidentally over-heard, had also played its part in convincing Sara that a bond of some kind existed between the two.

On her way to bed, Sara had wandered into the parlor, searching for her book. The room was empty, the lights dimmed. Olivia and Sylvia had evidently moved out onto the veranda, where Sara could hear them through the open doors, conversing quietly. Sara had certainly not meant to eavesdrop. She had been drifting about the room, her mind still on her quarrel with Felix, when the word 'poet' had arrested her attention.

Now Sara had a passion for poems. She

hoarded odd lines and phrases in her memory, guarding them jealously, taking them out from time to time to gloat over and polish, in the same way others delight in a favorite piece of jewelry. So when Sylvia had started talking about poetry, it was as though someone had unconsciously stretched out a hand in friendship, a hand she could not bear to ignore.

"Did you know," Sylvia had said suddenly, "that my father was a poet, as well as a teacher?"

"A poet?" Olivia had responded, surprised. "Why, no I didn't. You've told me so little about your parents."

"He published a volume of verse once, shortly after leaving Avonlea. He never published any more. Poor father. I think life disappointed him."

"What about your mother? Did she like poetry?"

"Heavens, no. Mother didn't care one whit for poetry. She died when I was born, you know. Father loved all poetry, though. And music too. *Greensleeves* was one of his favorite songs. That's why I love it so. When I was a little girl, he used to sing me to sleep with it. As I grew older, we would sing it together. I miss him terribly since his death, Olivia. He was all I had in the world to care about."

Sylvia had broken down then and Sara had

slipped silently upstairs, feeling her own father's absence weighing heavily on her heart. Yet, despite her longing for her father, she felt a small gleam of happiness. She could tell by Sylvia's tone that Sylvia shared her father's love of poetry. If that were so, then Sylvia was a potential soul mate. The thought that she and Sylvia Grey had more in common than a taste for Parisian-designed clothes had made Sara smile to herself as she turned over to go to sleep.

Now, as the dawn crept in through her open window, she realized that the emotion she had seen on Miss Lloyd's face as Sylvia sang, had its root not just in the loveliness of Sylvia's voice, but in the song itself. Clearly, *Greensleeves* meant just as much to Miss Lloyd as it had to Sylvia's father. Could Miss Lloyd have known him when he was a young teacher in Avonlea? Could she have loved him?

Too excited by this sudden insight to remain lying in bed any longer, Sara jumped up and began to dress.

Chapter Ten

The sun was climbing over the horizon as Sara approached the forbidding black gates of Miss

Lloyd's property. Even in the strong, clear light of early morning, it was impossible to repress a tiny shiver of fear. There was something daunting and dark about the place, something lost and lonesome and cold. Again, she found herself remembering Miss Lloyd's claim that the place was cursed. A phrase the old lady had used, 'consecrated by human blood,' rose unbidden in Sara's mind.

"Sara Stanley," she chided herself. "Don't just stand here dithering. Where's your natural gumption, as Aunt Hetty calls it?"

Giving herself a good shake, she slipped through the gate and up the long winding driveway.

As luck would have it, Miss Lloyd had just opened the door and taken a few steps towards a basket, which stood on the front steps, when Sara walked bravely up between the two stone lions.

"Go away," snapped the old lady, abandoning the basket and darting back into the house.

"I merely came," said Sara deliberately, "to inform you how much your mayflowers delighted Miss Grey."

Old Lady Lloyd paused in the very act of slamming the door. The words 'Miss Grey' seemed to have had the effect of a giant foot placed in the doorway.

"What on earth can you be thinking of, child? Have you transferred the Lloyd curse onto your own head now?"

"You don't care about no-one. No-one but yourself and all them dead people."

"What's the point of being young, if one can't be silly?"

Her heart gave a great, frightened leap, as someone rapped loudly on the front door.

"I have no idea what you're talking about," she replied, pushing the door open very slightly.

"She has a beautiful voice, don't you think?" asked Sara, advancing a step or two.

Miss Lloyd gazed at her. She seemed somehow defenseless. "Why are you so determined to pester me?"

"All I want, Miss Lloyd," answered Sara, recognizing the truth as she spoke it, "is to be your friend."

The old lady searched Sara's face for what seemed at least a minute. Then she made up her mind. "Come in and be quick about it," she said, holding the door wide open, "but not a word of this to anyone."

This time when the huge front door thundered shut behind her, Sara did not feel like a prisoner, but rather as if a rare treasure was about to be revealed to her.

Miss Lloyd ushered Sara along the hall and into the same cobweb-draped room she had seen through the window on the morning of her first visit.

From her new vantage point, Sara had a much clearer view. She looked with interest at several imposing portraits, hanging on the walls. It occurred to her that Miss Lloyd must have a wealth of family stories to tell, stories at least as macabre as those with which she had tried to terrify Sara on the day she had caught her in the garden. Fear or no fear, Sara had an insatiable appetite for good stories. Now that her knee had healed and she was no longer frightened of Miss Lloyd, the prospect of hearing a well-told tale filled her with pleasure. She wondered whether the old lady might be encouraged to recount more thrilling episodes from her family's past.

"I did so enjoy hearing about your ancestors the other day, Miss Lloyd," she prompted. "They seem to have led such colorful lives."

Miss Lloyd was staring up at a portrait of a plump-cheeked young woman with red hair. Her lips worked soundlessly.

"That's my Great-Aunt Sarah Lloyd," she finally brought out, her voice hoarse, as though unused to talking. "Such beautiful hair she had, and very proud of it she was too. Oh yes, much too vain for her own good. One night when she was brushing it in the north wing it caught fire from her candle and she ran shrieking down the hall wrapped in flames."

"Was she...?" Sara didn't quite like to use the expression 'burnt to a cinder'. It seemed far too irreverent.

"No, she did not burn to death, but she lost all her hair. And all her beauty along with it. She never went out of the house from that night to the day of her death, fifty years later." The old lady eyed Sara solemnly. "All part of the curse, my dear...all part of the curse." She moved on to the next portrait.

Sara decided to take the bull by the horns. She took a deep breath. "Miss Lloyd, I was wondering whether Sylvia Grey's father ever visited this house?"

The effect of her question on Miss Lloyd was immediate. The old lady swayed and had to grasp the mantelpiece for support. "Never you mind who came here and who did not," she rapped out, as soon as she had recovered. She gave Sara a sharp look. "What do you know about...about Richard Grey, you little minx?"

"I know he taught school here many years ago and that he spoke of his stay in Avonlea as the golden time in his life."

Miss Lloyd said nothing. Her beautiful, bony hands nervously twisted the Victorian mourning brooch at her throat.

"Sylvia still grieves for him, you know. She's all alone in the world now. Her mother died when she was born."

Still Miss Lloyd said nothing. Turning her back on Sara, she gazed unseeing into the huge mirror above the empty fireplace.

Behind her, Sara too looked into the mirror. And as she looked, she suddenly saw the room as it must once have been. It was not, it dawned on her, a drawing room at all, but a ballroom. In this very room, lit by hundreds of candles on glittering chandeliers, handsome young couples must have waltzed to the strains of a small orchestra. She could see a raised platform in one corner, where the orchestra would have played, safe above the whirling, whipping skirts of elegant young ladies, as they spun around the long, gracious room on the arms of their partners. Round and round they must have twirled, their eyes gleaming in the soft light, the scent from the flowers in their hair wafting upwards in the heat from the fireplace.

In the dim mirror, Sara's eyes returned to the present and met Miss Lloyd's. "I'm sorry," she said quietly. "It must be difficult to speak of a past which, I imagine, was filled with music and romance."

"There was music...once," acknowledged Miss Lloyd with difficulty. "Music and laughter and some...romance."

She looked so frail, yet dignified, standing there in the forgotten room, with its once-splendid furniture shrouded in sheets, and bare patches on the walls where valuable paintings had once hung, that Sara's heart filled with sympathy. "I couldn't help notice that you've had to sell some of your treasures, Miss Lloyd," she said impulsively, remembering her own misery when her father's possessions had been stripped from their home. "I too have endured the humiliation of—"

But she had gone too far. Miss Lloyd wheeled, her eyes flashing. "Hold your tongue. How dare you speak to me of private matters. I will not tolerate any further meddling into my affairs!"

Dimly, Sara recognized that she had ventured too close to something guarded and wounded within Miss Lloyd. It would be some time before she recognized that the wall she had stumbled against so clumsily was pride.

It was time to leave, she told herself. She had no wish to anger the old lady any further. Yet she lingered. She had still not discovered the connection between Miss Lloyd and Sylvia Grey.

Warily, she tried again. "We were just discussing next Sunday," she remarked, as though embarking on a completely different topic of conversation, "at Rose Cottage. It appears Miss Grey has agreed to sing a solo in church." She turned to Miss Lloyd. "Perhaps you might be interested in coming?"

The old lady made no answer and for a second

Sara feared she had offended her again. In fact, Miss Lloyd had temporarily forgotten all about Sara. All her thoughts, feelings and wishes were submerged in a very whirlpool of desire to hear Sylvia sing once more. But to hear her, she would have to go to church, and her pride rebelled at the thought of appearing in church in her out-of-date clothes. "I couldn't, I simply couldn't bring myself," she murmured, desire battling with pride. "I have no fit clothes to go to church in. Everyone would know that Margaret Lloyd had been reduced to wearing outmoded, shabby silks. I, who once set the fashion on this Island."

Her eyes fell on Sara. "But you, child...you'll be going, won't you? You could return next week and describe her to me. Would you do that?"

Sara thought quickly. Although Miss Lloyd had as good as confessed her strong interest in Sylvia, she had not yet revealed the reason behind it. Perhaps she would never reveal it. Perhaps Sylvia would return whence she came, knowing nothing of the old lady's secret attachment to her. What was the good of all this secrecy, Sara wondered. Surely it would be better for Miss Lloyd to see Sylvia and for Sylvia to see her? Ignoring the pleading in the old lady's voice, Sara shook her head. "I'm sorry, Miss Lloyd. I refuse to say another word about Sylvia. If you wish to find out more about her, you will have to do so yourself."

Thwarted, Miss Lloyd glared at this odd, unbiddable creature whom she had admitted into her home. "Why, you...you impertinent young wren! How dare you adopt such a tone with me. It's outrageous! It's unspeakable! It's—"

A fit of coughing interrupted her invective. By the time she had recovered, Sara was turning the handle of the front door. "Goodbye, Miss Lloyd." She smiled sweetly. "I look forward to seeing you in church on Sunday."

Miss Lloyd scowled. "Don't you dare breathe a word to anyone of my reduced circumstances. You hear me, girl?"

But Sara was already skipping down the steps, the feeling of a morning's work well done bubbling up inside her.

Chapter Eleven

The following Sunday the Avonlea congregation enjoyed a mild sensation. Just as the first organ chords of Sylvia's solo sounded, the doors to the church opened, admitting a stream of light into the packed building. Very slowly, looking neither to left nor right, Old Lady Lloyd entered into public view. Erect and dignified, one hand clutching her silver-topped cane, she made her way to the long-unoccupied Lloyd family pew, as though supremely unconscious of the whispers and stares she evoked around her.

Although she appeared unmoved, the old lady's soul was writhing within her. She recalled the reflection she had seen in her mirror before she left—the old black silk in the mode of forty years ago and the queer little bonnet of shirred black satin. Sitting upright in her pew, she thought how absurd she must look in the eyes of the world.

As a matter of fact, she did not look in the least absurd. Some women might have—but the old lady's stately distinction of carriage and figure was so subtly commanding that it did away with the consideration of clothing altogether. But Miss Lloyd did not know this. She sat there, wishing she had not come at all and feeling humiliated to her very bones.

Then all at once Sylvia's voice soared through the church like the very soul of melody. Nobody in Avonlea had ever listened to such a voice, except Old Lady Lloyd herself, who, in her youth, had heard enough good singing to enable her to be a tolerable judge. As she listened, her first impression was confirmed. This girl had a great gift—a gift that would some day bring her fame and fortune, if it could be duly trained and developed.

The afternoon sunshine fell over Sylvia's hair like a halo. The old lady sat and gazed at Richard Grey's daughter, feeling all her foolish thoughts, born of vanity and morbid pride, melt away as if they had never been. Into her mind flooded instead a wave of memories of Sylvia's father so strong and vivid that her head reeled. It came to her then, as Sylvia's voice echoed through the church, that forty years ago she had held happiness in her hand like a flower. Forty years ago she had flung it away. It would never be hers again. From that moment when she had rejected happiness, her feet were turned from youth to walk down a valley filled with shadow, to a lonely, eccentric old age. Tears welled up in her eyes. She told herself she must not break down. She *could not* break down in front of all these people. Yet the thought of all she had lost stabbed at her heart, destroying her self-control. Overwhelmed by sadness, she stood up and walked from the church.

Sara had noted Miss Lloyd's entrance with a thrill of satisfaction. The dignity of the old lady's deportment, as she took her place in her pew, impressed her. There was something splendid and regal about her, Sara decided, something courageous. She felt proud to be associated, even in a small way, with such gallantry. She was just beginning to imagine how she would introduce Sylvia to Miss Lloyd after the service, when she saw Miss Lloyd rise and hurriedly leave the church.

Slipping from her pew, Sara followed the old lady. She hoped Miss Lloyd had not been taken ill. On the steps she paused, blinking in the strong sunlight. Miss Lloyd was a black shadow hurrying along the street. Sara had to run to catch up with her. "Miss Lloyd, wait!" she called.

Miss Lloyd turned, her cheeks wet with tears.

"What's wrong, Miss Lloyd?" Sara felt seriously worried now. Miss Lloyd's face was white as paper. "Are you ill?"

The bright sun beat down on Miss Lloyd as she stood in the middle of the deserted Sunday street. She said nothing. She seemed hardly to hear Sara.

"Didn't you like Miss Grey's singing?"

The old lady dragged her thoughts back forty years. She stared at Sara, barely recognizing her. "What's wrong? What's wrong?" Her voice was muffled by tears. "Everything's wrong. Everything. I should never have come."

Without another word she turned and hastened away.

Sara gazed after her, on the point of tears herself. Everything had seemed to be going so well. If only she could have persuaded Miss Lloyd to stay until Sylvia could meet her. But far from seeming to want to make Sylvia's acquaintance, Miss Lloyd seemed to be running away from her.

Bitterly disappointed, Sara made her way back into church.

When the service was over, the congregation flocked out onto the front steps of the church. Further down the path, the Avonlea gossips gathered like hungry hens to peck away at Miss Lloyd's reputation.

"To think she once prided herself on her fashion sense," clucked Mrs. Kimball, the butcher's wife, rustling her own fine feathers complacently. "I declare I wouldn't be caught dead wearing such dated old rags to church."

"Doesn't darken the church door for umpteen years and then hightails out of it, soon's she sets foot in her pew," sniffed Mrs. Sloane.

"That's because some people think they're too good to walk the same earth as the rest of us, let alone attend the same church," pronounced Hetty King who, while claiming she disapproved of gossip, still felt an obligation to help people interpret it correctly.

Meanwhile, Sylvia Grey had been surrounded by a throng of admirers, foremost among whom was Mrs. Lawson, president of the Avonlea Ladies' Guild. Bustling as close to Sylvia as she could possibly get without knocking her down, she took her hand in hers.

"I was deeply, deeply moved, Miss Grey," she murmured in a low, vibrant voice. "And as for the collection plates, why, they simply overflowed!" Her eyes filled, as if in sympathy with the plates. Dabbing at them with the daintiest of lace handkerchiefs, she inclined her head towards Sylvia's ear.

"Miss Grey," she confided, "our Guild would like to sponsor you for the Cameron musical competition. With a voice like yours, the prize is as good as won. The ladies would be thrilled to have you as their candidate, believe me!" The long feathers on Mrs. Lawson's hat bobbed their agreement. Sylvia was obliged to move back a pace to prevent her ear being tickled.

"Why, Mrs. Lawson," she smiled. "How kind of you. You quite take my breath away."

Mrs. Lawson twinkled at Sylvia, satisfied with the effect of her little announcement. She stepped closer, her feathers prancing. "I rather hoped I might. Now...," her nose twitched roguishly, "let me fill you in on all the details...."

Chapter Twelve

Some time later Sylvia burst into Rose Cottage with her news. "Girls! Girls!" she screamed, jumping up and down with excitement. "Just wait till you hear!"

Olivia and Sara were in the kitchen preparing sandwiches for tea. Hetty had not yet returned home from the Altar Guild.

"What on earth's the matter?" asked Olivia, almost dropping the teapot in her surprise.

"My dears, this could mean the opportunity of a lifetime for me!" Sylvia's eyes positively danced in her head. She took the teapot from Olivia's grasp and placed it on the table. "Now don't look so worried, Olivia, dear. I bring good tidings this time. Just sit down and listen."

Her eyes glued to her friend's face, Olivia felt for a chair and sat down obediently. Sylvia took up her position in the middle of the room.

"I gather everyone around here has heard of Andrew Cameron, the millionaire?"

Olivia nodded solemnly. Sara hesitated. She *had* heard the name Cameron recently, only she couldn't quite remember where, or in what connection.

"Well," continued Sylvia, barely pausing for breath, "it seems Mr. Cameron sends one young singer away to Europe every year, for a thorough musical education under the best teachers. And the Avonlea Ladies' Guild, bless its kindly heart, has offered to sponsor me as its candidate for the Cameron scholarship this year!"

Olivia jumped up to hug her friend.

"Why, Sylvia, how wonderful! It seems like the answer to our prayers."

Sylvia hugged her back. "Doesn't it, though? But let's not count our chickens before they're hatched. I still have to win."

"I know you'll win. I know it right down to my very bones. Why, your voice has the power to make everyone happy, even the most demanding of judges."

An image of Miss Lloyd's face, wet with tears, appeared before Sara's eyes. Sylvia's voice, it seemed, had the power to make people sad, as well as happy. It occurred to Sara that she had never seen Miss Lloyd smile. How wonderful that would be, she reflected, to bring a smile to the old lady's face.

"Sylvia," she said abruptly. "Do you know who came to hear you in church today?"

"Why, no, Sara. Who?"

"Everyone around here calls her Old Lady

Lloyd," replied Sara, watching Sylvia's face carefully.

Sylvia stared at Sara. "Not...Miss...Margaret...Lloyd?" she asked in a low voice.

"Yes. Do you know her? Do you?"

Sylvia sat down abruptly. The look of happiness, which radiated from her face just seconds ago, had flown.

"I know who she is, of course. But I imagined she must have died years ago." She gazed down at her hands. "If she knew who I was, I don't believe she'd ever have come to hear me sing."

"Please, Sylvia," begged Sara. "Please come to meet her. Please."

Sylvia gazed first at Sara, then at Olivia. She sighed. "I suppose I should tell you the whole sad story," she said. "Only I'm not sure where to begin."

She began on the buggy, as they rode over to see Miss Lloyd. It was quite a simple story really.

Long ago—more than forty years ago—Sylvia's father had come to Avonlea to teach school for the summer term. He had been a young college student at the time, a shy, dreamy, handsome fellow with literary ambitions. At a party at the Lloyd mansion, he had met and fallen in love with pretty, wilful, high-spirited Margaret Lloyd.

Margaret stood to inherit a huge fortune from her father. But Richard Grey had no wish to be labeled a fortune hunter. The young couple became engaged in secret, at Richard's request. He hoped to make his own fortune before publicly claiming Margaret's hand.

After their blissful summer he left Avonlea, promising to write to his beloved Margaret every day. He had honored his promise. But then, suddenly, Margaret's letters had ceased. Richard had written many times, asking for an explanation to her silence. His letters had been returned to him unopened. Sick at heart, he had returned to Avonlea and attempted to see her. But Margaret Lloyd had given strict instructions to the servants to admit no one. He had been turned away from her door.

This last rejection convinced Richard Grey that Margaret Lloyd had stopped loving him. Heartbroken, he had left the country and traveled around Europe. Many years later, he married Sylvia's mother.

"But I've always known," concluded Sylvia, "that Margaret Lloyd was his one, great love. After father's death, I found her letters to him, every single one. He had kept them, all those years."

There was a moment's silence. Then Sara gave

a huge, satisfied sigh. "My goodness," she murmured, "what a perfectly romantic story."

"There've been many times since father died," said Sylvia, "that I've thought of writing to Miss Lloyd. But each time I would ask myself: Why should she want to hear from the daughter of a man she stopped loving years ago? Besides, I had no idea whether she was alive or dead."

"I wonder...," mused Sara, "I wonder what made her letters stop?"

Alone in her cavernous dining room, Miss Margaret Lloyd seated herself at one end of the long mahogany table. The setting sun filtered through dusty windows, lighting up her frugal Sunday supper. It had been a trying day for the old lady and she had little appetite. The hands which rested on the fine old wood shook slightly. Her eyes stared listlessly at the empty wall. The fresh brown egg, which Peg had left for her that morning, remained untouched.

The unfamiliar sound of a buggy turning into her driveway and advancing towards the house caused her to stiffen in alarm. Wheels ground on the gravel, then stopped. Footsteps approached the house. They climbed the front steps. Her heart gave a great, frightened leap as someone rapped loudly at the front door.

She stood up and walked haltingly towards the hall.

"Miss Lloyd!"

It was the voice of that strange girl whose knee she had bandaged.

"Miss Lloyd, I've brought Sylvia Grey to see you."

Into the old lady's white face came a sudden faint stain of color, as if a rough hand had struck her cheek. She leaned against the wall, trembling.

"Whom have you brought, did you say?" Her voice carried weakly through the heavy door.

"I said Sylvia Grey, Miss Lloyd." Sara lifted the flap of the letter box and spoke through it. "She wants to meet you."

In the darkness of the hall Miss Lloyd leaned her forehead against the cool wall. She did not trust herself to reply.

A strange, yet familiar voice spoke up.

"Miss Lloyd," the voice said gently, "I am Richard Grey's daughter. Perhaps you remember him? He spoke of you often."

Remember him? Tears flooded the old lady's eyes. She could not speak. Richard's daughter was here, at her doorstep. *His* daughter. "And she might have been *my* daughter," she murmured to herself.

Oh, if only she could let her in! But she could

not. She could not have Richard's daughter know how low she had been brought. No, she could not bear her to know in what reduced circumstances the once proud Margaret Lloyd was forced to live.

"Miss Lloyd," Sara's voice spoke up again. "For heaven's sake, Miss Lloyd, open the door!" Rat-a-tat went the brass door knocker, RAT-A-TAT-A-TAT.

There was a murmur on the other side. Another voice spoke sharply.

"Stop it, Sara," the unfamiliar voice said. "We must respect her privacy. Now come away."

Footsteps descended the steps and mounted the buggy.

Miss Lloyd stumbled to the living room window and peered out. She was just in time to see a buggy disappearing down the driveway. In the back sat a slim, straight young woman. Her head, with its burnished copper hair, was turned longingly towards the closed front door.

With a sob, the old lady sank back against the wall. Her heart felt like lead within her. Richard's daughter had come to see her and she had turned her away.

Had she not stood at this same window forty years ago and watched, racked with grief, as Richard himself had been turned away, refused admittance by her own orders?

Had the years taught her nothing except how to close others out of her life?

Chapter Thirteen

It was the day of the Cameron competition. Sylvia had vocalized and practiced till even Felix knew every one of her songs by heart. Now she stood in front of Olivia's oval mirror, dressed in her dainty muslin gown, while Olivia, her eyes shining, her cheeks flushed with excitement, helped her adjust her white lace stole.

Hetty's raised voice could be heard advancing up the stairs. "If I can't see my face in those shoes of yours, Andrew, then I do not consider them polished! Felix King, I said wash behind BOTH ears! And hurry up, for pity's sake, or we'll be late." She bustled into the bedroom. "Would you girls kindly stop primping and hurry along or—" She stopped short, glaring at Olivia's pink cheeks. "Why, Olivia, you've too much color. People will think you're painted."

Olivia, who would no more have dreamed of applying paint to her flawless complexion than she would have considered swearing, flushed a deep crimson. Biting back an angry response, she spoke to her elder sister calmly. "I can tell your nerves are worn to a frazzle, Hetty. Now I don't want you to spoil this afternoon for the children by bossing them about."

"But—"

Olivia steered the agitated Hetty gently towards the door.

"We'll be down in two minutes. Why don't you ask Andrew to hitch up the buggy."

Hetty sniffed the air suspiciously. "Scent! Someone in this room's drenched with scent. I won't have it. It doesn't smell one bit respectable."

"Hetty, please. We'll be late."

With one final, outraged sniff, Hetty backed out of the room. Olivia closed the door firmly behind her.

Sylvia chuckled. "I do believe you're learning how to handle her at long last."

"She's right, though," replied Olivia, reaching for her hat. "If we don't hurry, we shall be horribly late."

Felix was lying in wait for Sara as she came down the stairs. His hair was plastered to his head with water. His neck smarted from a vigorous scrubbing administered by Aunt Hetty. "Aunt Hetty says I can so come in the buggy this time, Sara," he announced. "So don't you try and stop me."

Sara smoothed down the skirt of her blue taffeta dress. He wished she would smile at him. But she walked right by, without so much as a glance.

"I'll do whatever Aunt Hetty says," she replied. "But don't imagine for a moment that I forgive you."

A little wind sent plump white clouds scudding across the sky, as the group set out for Charlottetown. Normally, on an excursion such as this, the mood would have been merry, the laughter loud. But by this time they had all realized that time was pressing. The unspoken fear of arriving late at the concert dampened everyone's spirits.

For a while Felix sulked, because Sara had made a point of sitting as far away from him as possible. Then he forgot his resentment in trying to figure out how fast the buggy was going. It seemed to fly along the dusty road, creaking and groaning in protest all the way.

Aunt Hetty, who normally gripped the side and invoked the mercy of heaven if the horse so much as trotted, was now urging it into a frenzied gallop. According to the little watch pinned to her jacket, they were already ten minutes behind schedule. Unpunctuality was to Hetty as murder is to a hanging judge. "What kind of driver are you anyway, Andrew King?" she snapped, almost snatching the reins from him. "Can't you make that silly horse go any faster?"

Sylvia's eyes were shut and her lips moved. Cecily thought she must be reciting one of her songs to herself, but Sara knew she was praying. Suddenly she opened her eyes and reached out a gloved hand to Andrew.

"Please, Andrew," she whispered. "Please hurry. We just *can't* be late!"

Sylvia's word was Andrew's command. He crouched low over the straining horse, bullying it, coaxing it. Along the stony, rutted lane tore the old buggy, clouds of red dust whirling up around it.

Then it happened. With a loud snap, the front axle broke in two. A wheel went careening off into a ditch. Andrew reined in the startled horse just in time. Children tumbled over adults. Adults clutched the sides of the cart and gave themselves over to white-knuckled terror.

Suppressing a desire to yell rude words at the top of his voice, Andrew made a flying leap from the buggy and surveyed the scene. It was clear the damage could not be easily repaired.

Silence and dust settled over them. They

gazed at each other in despair, hearing the minutes tick away.

It was Aunt Hetty who took command. "Off to King Farm with you," she commanded Andrew. "Fetch your Uncle's buggy quick as you can."

As Andrew set off, heading back the way they had come, Hetty stood up in the cart, ignoring her shaking knees. She clambered over the side, adjusted her hat, and dusted off her skirt. "We'll have to put our best foot forward till Andrew catches up."

She jerked her head commandingly at the others, who sat, as if frozen, in the collapsed buggy. "Come on! Down you get, all of you! What did God give you feet for, if not to walk?"

Reaching up, she yanked first Cecily and then Felix out of the cart. One by one the others followed. Meekly, they set off along the lane in Aunt Hetty's wake.

They had been walking for what seemed like hours. The children had given up worrying about the time and plodded silently onwards, their heads bent. Olivia glanced over at Sylvia. Her pretty dress was stained with dust from the road. Her white stole trailed disconsolately behind her. Her hat was crooked and her hair was coming down at the back. But it was the look of defeat in her friend's eyes which made

Olivia's heart contract.

"We might still make it, if Andrew comes soon," she whispered, slipping her arm around Sylvia's shoulders. "And if we don't, well, maybe it's all for the best. Remember what Shakespeare said, Sylvia: 'there's a divinity that shapes our ends'."

"Divinity, my auntie!" snorted Hetty. "If you hadn't spent so much time titivating, we wouldn't have been late in the first place."

A screech of delight from Felix cut off Olivia's reply. Andrew was tearing down the lane on Uncle Alec's buggy.

Maybe, just maybe, they would be in time after all.

Mrs. Lawson met them as they scurried up the stairs of the town hall. The look she threw them quenched their every last hope.

Sylvia began to apologize immediately, but Hetty cut her off. "When does the girl go on, Elvira?"

"Why, you're much too late! I can't imagine what you were thinking, Hetty King. Mr. Cameron's already reached his decision."

Mrs. Lawson's prominent eyes gazed reproachfully at Sylvia. "What an abysmal shame, my dear. The girl who won isn't half as talented as you. But then, she did have punctuality on her side."

Hetty's face burned. She felt herself included in Elvira Lawson's rebuke. To be accused of unpunctuality, and in public too! It would be many a year before Hetty would forget such humiliation.

A burst of applause sounded from the auditorium. As one, they all moved towards the open door, which led into the crowded hall.

On the brightly lit stage a dowdy young woman blinked her eyes and curtsied to the audience. As she straightened up, a well-groomed man in a dark suit strode up to her. In one hand he carried an envelope.

Sara stared at him, noting the aura of sleek prosperity which hung about him like a fragrance. Something about the way he extended the white envelope towards the simpering young woman struck a chord in her memory. Where had she seen him before?

Mrs. Lawson nudged Sylvia. "Just think, my dear," she sighed, turning the knife skillfully in the wound. "That might have been you, standing up there, receiving the award from Mr. Cameron himself."

Sylvia's eyes filled with tears. But she blinked them away fiercely. "I'm sure the young lady deserves her award, Mrs. Lawson," she replied.

Raising her dusty, gloved hands, she joined in the applause.

Chapter Fourteen

Moonlight fell in a silvery shower over a sleeping Rose Cottage. A breeze rocked the spruce trees to sibilant sleep and the dark sky danced with a thousand stars.

In the soft starshine flooding her bedroom, Sara awoke. Night's blanket of silence seemed to cover the entire house. Yet she was sure some noise had wakened her.

Listening intently, she became aware of a small sound floating up from outside, a tiny, choked sound. It was the sound someone makes who wants to cry out loud, to weep and flail around. But fearful of disturbing others, the weeper makes do instead with dry, inward sobs. Only sometimes the quiet mourning escapes into the night and makes just the sort of high, gasping noise Sara had heard. She recognized it at once. Had she not wept herself to sleep in such a way many times, grieving for her absent father?

Pushing back her sheets, Sara rose and crept to the open window.

Down below she saw Olivia tiptoe onto the

veranda in her dressing gown. She was hurrying towards Sylvia, who sat crumpled up in a white chair, valiantly holding back her sobs.

"I'm so sorry, Olivia," she gasped, rumpling at her face with her handkerchief. "I did try not to wake you. But I'm such a rattle-brained creature, I can't even grieve without attracting attention."

"Oh, don't cry, Sylvia. Please don't." Olivia felt like weeping herself out of pure sympathy.

"I shouldn't, I know. It makes my nose swell. And there's nothing quite so unbecoming as a swollen nose, particularly if it's peasant-like to start with. But I can't help it, truly I can't. I was just so buoyed up about that competition."

"Perhaps if Mr. Cameron understood your circumstances, he might still consider you. He might, you know."

"No, Olivia, you said so yourself. 'The divinity that shapes our ends'—remember? Well, my divinity seems to have ordained me to be a schoolmarm, and that's that. Why should Mr. Cameron care about me? Nobody else does."

Sara was sorely tempted to lean out the window and call to Sylvia: "Miss Lloyd cares about you. I know she does."

But she knew she should not be listening to such a private conversation, and so she drew back inside and closed the window softly.

As she did so, it came to her suddenly where she had seen Mr. Cameron before. Of course! It was at Old Lady Lloyd's. How *could* she have forgotten! Into her brain flashed a picture of Andrew Cameron holding out an envelope to the old lady, who had drawn back in anger. She remembered it all quite clearly now. He and Miss Lloyd were cousins and he had offered to help her.

Sara climbed back into bed, hugging to herself a daring new plan of attack.

Chapter Fifteen

It was not yet quite light when Sara slipped out of Rose Cottage the next morning. She had dressed in the dark, for fear Aunt Hetty should hear her lighting her candle and demand to know why she was stirring so early.

Shadows lay thick as autumn leaves on the driveway, as Sara approached the Lloyd house. A squirrel darted across her path. It did not leap and bound in the air. Nor did it pause to examine her with quivering curiosity, as Avonlea squirrels are wont to do. Without one single extravagance of gesture, it darted into the undergrowth and was gone.

Small, sulky gray clouds huddled together over the forest. The air seemed still and sticky. A storm must be coming, Sara thought, as she banged loudly on the old lady's door.

"I've come about Sylvia, Miss Lloyd," she called, hearing a dry cough within. "She's in dire straits. I believe you're the only person who can help her."

Miss Lloyd opened the door a crack. She seemed paler and more frail than Sara remembered her. "Say what's on your mind quickly. Then be off," she barked.

"I'm afraid it's rather difficult to say quickly," said Sara, knowing she must choose her words carefully. "You see, Sylvia was hoping to win the Cameron competition. But our buggy broke and we arrived too late. And now Sylvia's heart is broken, too. I thought...that is, I was hoping...you might ask Andrew Cameron to...to...reconsider." Sara's voice faltered. She gazed pleadingly up at the old lady.

Miss Lloyd gripped the door. This child was treading on dangerous ground. The very mention of Andrew Cameron's name seemed to cause the bones of the Lloyd family skeletons to jangle in their closet. She pulled the door shut. But the child had grasped it and was holding it open.

"Please, Miss Lloyd?"

Miss Lloyd sighed. She was tired, much too tired to have to deal with difficult children. But the child was staring at her imploringly, willing her with her eyes to answer.

"I'd rather die than ask that thieving cousin of mine to do me a favor," she replied finally.

"But he seemed like such a kind man the day he visited you."

"Kind! Humbug. He'd steal your grave, soon as look at you!"

"Then why was he trying to be so generous with you?" Sara was genuinely perplexed.

"Out of guilt! Nothing more!" The old lady moved as though to wrench the door from Sara's grasp, but Sara quickly reached out and held her wrist.

"Please, Miss Lloyd, I don't understand."

Miss Lloyd could feel Sara's hand through the thin silk at her wrist. It was a long time since anyone had reached out to her, touched her. She relented slightly.

"It's quite simple to understand, child. He once advised my father to invest his fortune in an enterprise which failed. My father was ruined. But Andrew Cameron emerged unscathed. He became a wealthy man—at my father's expense."

"But he did want to make amends. I heard him offer to help you."

Miss Lloyd's face hardened. "We may have nothing else. But we Lloyds still have our pride, my dear."

There was that word again. Pride. The old rumor about Miss Lloyd darted into Sara's head: "rich, mean and proud." Well, she was neither rich nor mean—Sara could testify to that. But proud she certainly seemed.

Quite suddenly, as if that word contained the last piece of a puzzle, Sara understood. "So *that's* why you stopped writing to Sylvia's father," she burst out.

Miss Lloyd's lip trembled. "I...I couldn't have him marry me out of pity. No. That was out of the question. It was no one's business to know how poor we'd suddenly become."

"But you broke his heart."

"And mine. I destroyed my own happiness as well." Miss Lloyd gazed bleakly about her. The whole of her present seemed overshadowed by her past. "It's this house, you see. This cursed house! It's full of heartbreak."

But Sara had seen through the curse. There was no going back.

"That's just an excuse, Miss Lloyd, and you know it. The real curse is your own stubborn pride."

Miss Lloyd drew back as if Sara had struck

her. "How DARE you!"

"No, listen, Miss Lloyd, please. Forget about your pride. If you loved her father once, then help Sylvia now. She needs you."

Miss Lloyd raised her cane in fury. "Get out!" she gasped. "For once and for all, leave me alone." Stepping back into the house, she slammed and bolted the door.

Chapter Sixteen

Peg Bowen glanced skyward. Huge, black-edged clouds squatted overhead, blocking out the sun. The air felt leaden. The clouds seemed to press downward on the earth, as though to crush it.

Peg wiped her arm across her brow. Trouble's brewing, she thought to herself. Picking up the herbs she had gathered, she dropped them into her basket. As she moved off through the Lloyd graveyard, she noticed old Miss Lloyd approaching from the house.

Peg stared. Something was wrong. Normally the old lady bore herself proudly, barely leaning on the cane she sometimes carried. Every action was precise, well-timed, almost graceful. Yet now her movements seemed random, confused. She half lurched towards Peg, changed her mind, turned as if to go back to the house, then sat down suddenly by her father's grave.

Peg removed the pipe from her mouth. "You'd best go back inside," she called over. "There's a storm movin' in."

The old lady paid no attention. Her eyes roamed restlessly around the graveyard. "Nothing matters any more," she whispered.

Peg's eyes narrowed. "Is that so?" she asked sternly. "Well, let me tell you, you'll lie under the sod soon enough, if you keep on the way you're going. There'll be time enough then for self-pity."

Distractedly, Miss Lloyd ran her hand along the cold marble of her father's tombstone. "Don't talk like that, Peg."

But the time for such talk had come. Peg knew it, and was not to be stopped. "Who'll carve your name on the stone then, eh? Who'll weep by your grave side? No one." She almost spat the word out. "Because no one'll give a tinker's damn about you."

"It's not true."

"It is so true. Why should anyone care? You don't care about no one. No one but yourself and all them dead people." Peg pointed a bony finger in the direction of the Lloyd graves. "If you don't do somethin' about it soon, then all you'll get's an unmarked, unwept grave. An' let me tell you, it'll be all you deserve. All you're fit for!"

Miss Lloyd stood up. Her wide, frightened eyes searched Peg's face. Peg stared back at her, unblinking.

Then Miss Lloyd turned and half ran, half stumbled from the graveyard. But she did not run towards the sheltering house, she ran away from it.

At that precise moment a bolt of lightning flashed against the pitch-black sky, followed by a savage growl. Angry clouds burst over the trees, sending rain spattering in every direction.

Peg Bowen followed the old lady as far as the gate and noted the direction she took. Again, the old proverb danced in her brain. *For every evil under the sun...*

"Ay," she thought to herself. "Either we find that remedy now, or not at all."

But she felt uneasy all that afternoon. And by nightfall she had determined to take matters into her own hands.

Chapter Seventeen

Old Lady Lloyd stumbled along the cliff path, her soul sick within her. It was a long walk to Charlottetown and she had left without money or food. But walk it she would. For had not that Sara girl told her that Sylvia needed her help? It was in her power to send Richard Grey's daughter to Europe for her musical education—she knew that. She had no doubt whatsoever that if she, Margaret Lloyd, asked Andrew Cameron to assist Sylvia, it would be done. No, what sickened her was that she had hesitated. She had not wanted to crush and conquer her pride in order to ask a favor of the man who had wronged her so bitterly.

Peg was right, she had not thought of others. She had thought only of herself, only of her pride, which had grown so thick and tangled it threatened to choke all other emotions. But now she would fight it, and in fighting, she would allow love to grow.

Love is a great miracle worker, and never had its power been more strongly shown than on that stormy day when old Miss Lloyd set out to walk all the way to Charlottetown for Sylvia's sake.

Rain danced down like a wild thing. Tall trees crouched over the lane, as if trying to shield their heads from the merciless pounding. All light had fled from the sky. Bushes and shrubs bent low and grieved, while water streamed from their prostrate forms.

From one side of the road to the other

stretched deep, frothy puddles. At first the old lady tried to step across each one. But soon she gave up and splashed blindly through. Long before she reached Bright River, her shoes were wet through and made loud squelching noises as she walked.

Some time out from Bright River, Mr. Harmon McIlroy, a passing farmer, offered her a lift in his truck wagon. Miss Lloyd struggled in gratefully. She was too tired to make conversation and Harmon had no idea who she was. But he thought she looked uncommonly white and peaked, "as if she hadn't slept a wink or eaten a bite for a week," he told his wife later at dinner time.

When they reached the fork in the road where he turned off, Harmon courteously offered her shelter at his farm. But the old lady refused his offer. "Thank you no," she said, as she straightened her sodden shawl about her shoulders. "I must be in Charlottetown before nightfall."

Harmon helped her down from the wagon, waved goodbye and turned his team of grays homeward. "I wouldn't put a dog out in this weather," he muttered to himself, wondering what business affair could be of such supreme importance, as to bring an old lady out in so terrible a downpour.

By the time Miss Lloyd reached Charlotte-town, the rain had vented much of its anger. It fell listlessly, as though it had lost interest. Miss Lloyd still had two more miles to walk, for Andrew Cameron lived some distance out on the other side of town. She felt as if she were walking in a nightmare. Nothing mattered but that she force one foot in front of the other. Nothing mattered but that she make this enormous effort for Sylvia.

People passing by greeted her politely, or stared out of the corners of their eyes. She did not see them at all. Memory alone guided her over the last half-mile, for the sun had appeared quite suddenly from behind the thick mass of cloud, and its sudden brightness caused her eyes to mist over.

As she staggered up the driveway, which appeared as impeccable and well-manicured as Andrew Cameron himself, she realized that a burning heat had taken the place of her former chilliness. "How hot that sun must be," she thought as she reached out a shaking hand and knocked on the door.

Chapter Eighteen

Polly Deane had not been in the service of Mr. Cameron for long and there were many aspects of her new employment which delighted her. Her starched white uniform with its frilly cap, which stood to attention on top of her blonde head, filled her with pride. So too did the front hall, with its gleaming mirrors and fresh-cut flowers. She admired the important sweep of the drive as it curved around Mr. Cameron's front steps, and the way the gardeners kept the grass trimmed to within an inch of its life.

Even now, after six weeks of playing front parlor maid, the sound of the heavy brass knocker, which she always thought of possessively as 'hers', made Polly's blue eyes shine. For then she would have to stop whatever menial task she was performing in the kitchen, straighten her little white apron, flick out her hair at the sides and sail up the back stairs, saying to Cook with an important air, "Excuse me, Cook, that's for me."

She was still smiling as she opened the imposing front door on this rain-washed afternoon. Her hand on the latch, she paused, feeling her smile falter and her eyes begin to stare, in just the way her mother had warned her against. For there on the doorstep stood, or rather leaned, a wrinkled old lady, garbed entirely in shabby black. Water dripped from her hat, her shawl, her skirts, her gloves. Her eyes were closed. Her head was propped against one of the stone pilasters. She looked, as Polly whispered to the under-house-parlor-maid later that night, "for all the world as if she had drink taken."

Polly was just about to give the old lady a piece of her mind, when the woman opened her eyes and spoke.

"I should like," she whispered, in what Polly instantly recognized as ladylike accents, "to speak to Mr. Andrew Cameron."

Then she swayed and staggered forward, her whole body shaken by coughs. She would have fallen straight onto Polly's beautifully polished hardwood floor, had Polly not jumped forward and caught her. "Mr. Cameron! Mr. Cameron! Come quick, sir!" she screamed.

Mr. Cameron came dashing out from the drawing room.

"Cousin Margaret!" he exclaimed, in a voice in which amazement, delight and concern were all mixed up together.

With some difficulty Polly and Mr. Cameron contrived to half carry, half drag the shivering woman into the drawing room, where they placed her gently on the settee in front of the fire.

"Quickly, Polly, fetch a blanket," ordered Mr. Cameron as his clumsy fingers tried to remove the dripping stole from the old lady's shoulders.

His cousin raised her hand, as if warding off his help. She seemed to have something of the utmost importance on her mind. "I have come," she coughed, straining to sit upright, although her whole body shook with fever, "I have come to ask for your help, Andrew Cameron."

"Yes. Yes, of course," he answered soothingly, wondering if he dared unpin her sodden hat. "Now if you'll just lie back and rest, dear cousin Margaret...."

With enormous difficulty she straightened herself. She waved him away with a waterlogged glove. "Not for myself, you understand. But for Sylvia...Sylvia Grey."

As she uttered these last two words, the old lady smiled, a smile of such sweetness that Andrew Cameron felt tears start to his eyes.

"Why, Margaret!" he exclaimed, as it came to him that he had never before seen her smile.

But Margaret Lloyd did not hear him. She had fallen back against the settee, her eyes closed, her breathing labored.

"The doctor, Polly, quickly! Fetch the doctor!" shouted Mr. Cameron, suddenly fearful lest the cousin he had thought returned, was now lost to him forever.

Chapter Nineteen

Although the rain had eased off towards evening, water still clung to tree and bush, as Peg Bowen made her way to Rose Cottage. The moon had risen, and in its soft radiance raindrops shimmered like pearls strung from the limbs of the peach trees. Peg's hat and shoulders gleamed damply. Her tangled, grizzled hair fell unkemptly around her face. She scowled as she strode, and her fierce brown eyes held no friendly light. Any child, meeting her thus in the moonlight, might have been forgiven for believing her to be truly the Witch of Avonlea.

Such indeed were Sara's first thoughts on scrambling to her window after waking to the sound of pebble after pebble bouncing against the panes.

Peering out into the darkness, her eyes had met the burning eyes of Peg. Her initial impulse was to slam the window shut and jump back into bed, pulling the covers up tightly around her ears. But there was a look in those eyes, a steady, piercing look which held her rooted to the ground.

Although Peg spoke quietly, her words reached Sara clearly as she stood shivering in her night-gown.

"I come to tell you," said Peg. "Miss Lloyd may need you. Best you go after her, you and that singing girl."

"After her? Wh...where is she?"

"Over to Charlottetown. Takin' up on an old debt."

"Charlottetown? You mean she went to see Mr. Cameron?"

"Aye. Go to her now. And don't forget to take the singing girl. Them as belongs together must stay together. You hear me? Then go now, go on!" Without another word Peg turned and melted away into the trees.

Forgetting her fear, Sara leaned from the window to call her back. But Peg had vanished into the misty, moon-spangled night.

It was all very well, Sara reflected rather grumpily, for someone with Peg Bowen's special powers to wander in from the night and order people off to Charlottetown immediately. Just let her try confronting Aunt Hetty in the wee hours of the morning. Just let her try explaining to a rudely awakened, sleep-rumpled maiden aunt why a trip to Charlottetown had become such a pressing need.

Aunt Hetty had been neither impressed nor amused by Peg Bowen's mysterious message. "Charlottetown, my granny!" she had snorted, shaking her head so vigorously that her nightcap had slipped down over one eye, lending her such an odd, lopsided look, Sara found it hard not to smile. "It's a wonder she didn't offer to fly you there on her broom."

Luckily, Sylvia had come to Sara's rescue. In unusually firm tones she had explained to Aunt Hetty that Miss Lloyd was almost a member of her family and that it was her duty to hasten to her side in Charlottetown.

Duty was a cherished word in Aunt Hetty's lexicon. She had grudgingly given her consent, on the condition that Olivia accompany them. When Olivia had pointed out quite reasonably that the train didn't leave from Bright River till nine o'clock the following morning and that they could therefore all go back to bed, Aunt Hetty had brightened considerably.

"Back to bed then, the lot of you," she ordered. "Get your beauty sleep while you can. The Lord knows, you all need it."

The next minute she had stumped off to bed, taking her candle with her. Left in the dark, Sara, Olivia and Sylvia had no choice but to follow her.

The following morning they had taken the train to Charlottetown, where they had sought out the residence of Mr. Andrew Cameron.

On seeing them, Mr. Cameron's tired face had glowed with relief. "Thank heavens you've come," he said, drawing them all inside. "She had a terrible night last night, simply terrible. But the doctor says the worst is over. She's going to pull through."

He looked carefully at Sylvia as Sara introduced her. "So you're Sylvia Grey. She's been asking for you constantly."

Taking Sylvia's arm, he ushered her into the downstairs bedroom which had been hastily prepared for Miss Lloyd.

The old lady lay in bed, her face white as the lace pillows which surrounded her. She opened her eyes as Sylvia entered the room, and held out a thin hand. "Come closer," she murmured.

Sylvia approached the sick woman's bedside and took the frail hand in hers. Old Lady Lloyd gazed up at her, her eyes lingering with delight over every feature of the girl's fine face. "You look so much like your father," she said finally, with a satisfied sigh. Then, hesitating slightly, for she was not accustomed to asking for favors, "Would you sing for me, Sylvia?"

Sylvia looked down at the old lady propped on the pillows. She did not know why Miss Lloyd had exhausted herself struggling all the way to Charlottetown on foot in the rain, as Mr. Cameron had told them. All she knew was that in front of her lay the woman her father had once loved. He had cherished her memory as carefully as he had treasured her letters. He had never failed to speak of Avonlea in tones of warmth and regret. Whatever unknown cause had sundered him from Margaret Lloyd, he had borne her no grudges.

As a young girl, Sylvia had liked nothing better than to hear her father sing. Many times, as he sat at the piano, his light tenor voice filling the room, she had felt his thoughts return to Avonlea and that jewel of a summer he had shared with Margaret Lloyd. One song, in particular, reflected this mood. Raising her voice, she sang it now for both of them—for her father, whom she would never forget, and for the old lady, whom she loved because of him.

Oh, my love is like a red, red rose,
That's newly sprung in June.
My love is like a melody,
That's sweetly played in tune.
As fair art thou, my bonnie lass,
So deep in love am I,

And I will love thee still, my dear,
Till a' the seas gang dry.

Andrew Cameron listened to the pure, sweet tones and felt relief and gratitude wash over him. When his cousin Margaret had asked him to further the musical education of a young unknown called Sylvia Grey, he had consented instantly. Ever since, as a rash youth, he had urged his uncle to invest in a certain disastrous mining stock, he had been plagued by a sense of guilt towards the Lloyd family and Margaret in particular. He would have done anything in his power to silence that small, nagging voice which dwelt within his conscience and caused him many a sleepless night.

Since the day of his uncle's "financial accident" as his embarrassed nephew preferred to think of it, Andrew Cameron had hugged the narrow path of fiscal virtue. He had done his best to lead a good life, to establish himself as a pillar of the community. Though not particularly talented musically, he had always loved good singing. In establishing the Cameron musical scholarship, he liked to think that in his own small way he was contributing something of value to the larger world of song, as well as salving a troubled conscience. When awarding the prize, he had always attempted to select the most deserving amongst the candidates, wanting to be as unbiased and as principled as possible. Because of the debt he owed his cousin, however, he had been prepared to forsake principle. Now, as he heard Sylvia sing, he realized that this sacrifice of conscience would not be necessary. For here was a voice destined to grace the concert halls of the world. Here was a voice which on its own merits would lend prestige to the Cameron scholarship. Far from his doing his cousin or indeed Miss Grey a favor, it was Sylvia Grey who would confer a favor on him, were she to accept his offer of a scholarship. As the song ended he spoke his thoughts aloud.

"Miss Grey," he said, his voice hoarse with emotion, "I intend to do everything in my power to ensure that your voice receives the recognition it so richly deserves."

Sylvia Grey smiled at him gratefully, but it was clear that at present nothing was further from her mind than thoughts of career and ambition. Concern for the old lady, whom she now saw as the last remaining member of her family, was uppermost in her heart. Still holding Miss Lloyd's hand, she knelt by her bed.

"Sylvia, my dear," the old lady murmured, "I have gone through the valley of the shadow of death, and I have left pride and resentment behind me forever, I hope. I beg you to forgive a foolish old woman."

"There's nothing to forgive," whispered Sylvia. "You're part of my family now and that's all there is to it."

From her position behind Mr. Cameron, Sara saw a faint flush of color creep into the old lady's wan cheeks. Catching sight of Sara at that moment, Miss Lloyd beckoned her over. "Mine will be a very different sort of life from now on, Sara-girl," she promised, holding out her other hand to Sara, as though sealing a bargain.

Sara smiled at her, and then a queer sensation caught at her throat. For something close to miraculous was taking place in the old lady's face, which seemed to transform itself as Sara gazed. The once tightly pursed lips relaxed and turned upwards, the harsh lines softened, the cheeks grew rounder. In her delight Sara almost threw her arms around the old lady's neck. For Old Lady Lloyd was smiling, smiling as though a great new gladness of heart had welled up within her and was shining out through her eyes.

Chapter Twenty

It was weeks before Miss Lloyd was well enough to make the trip home from Charlottetown. In the meantime, word of her illness and of the circumstances in which she had lived spread like wildfire. Everyone knew now how poor the old lady really was. The story of how she had scrimped and saved, year after year, was discussed endlessly. Mindful of how they had shunned and dismissed her in the past, many of the people of Avonlea felt remorse fill their hearts. The gossips in particular repented of their harsh judgments.

"But who would have thought it?" remarked Aunt Hetty guiltily to the minister's wife. "Nobody ever dreamed that her father had lost all his money. It's shocking to think of the way she's lived all these years, often with not enough to eat—and going to bed in winter days to save fuel. Though I suppose if we had known we couldn't have done much for her, she's so desperately proud. But if she lives, and will let us help her, things will be different after this."

Aunt Hetty meant what she said. Before a day had passed, she had rounded up a small army of volunteers and put them to work scrubbing the neglected Lloyd mansion from top to bottom. Armed with mops, brooms and dusters, they attacked the countless gray layers of cobwebs, which generations of spiders had slaved to spin. As though erasing a great debt from their consciences, the old lady's neighbors worked tirelessly, sweeping, waxing, dusting, polishing and painting until the spiders were vanquished and the Lloyd mansion seemed to blaze forth with the renewed glory of its former days.

At his parents' insistence, Felix had been obliged to contribute some of his cherished savings towards a new window. His father had installed it. While doing so, Alec King had done his best to instill in his son a healthy respect for other people's property, whether those people were, as he put it, "under or over the sod."

On the day Andrew Cameron finally drove Miss Lloyd home in his fine new carriage, the whole King family assembled with several neighbors on the front steps to welcome her back.

Felicity had even gone so far as to dust down the carved lions guarding the entrance. Not to be outdone, Sara had woven a wreath of buttercups and daisies to crown each stone brow. But Aunt Hetty had removed these with one swift, disapproving flick of her broom. "Flowers inside the house are bad enough, but flowers on dumb beasts I will not tolerate. Where that child learnt such heathen practices I cannot fathom!"

Everyone cheered as Mr. Cameron helped his cousin out of the carriage. He had insisted on ordering her an elegant new gown for the occasion, and with her beautiful hair piled high on her head, her stately manner and the glow of happiness on her face, Miss Lloyd seemed to have been granted a new lease on life.

On Sylvia's arm, she walked about her gleaming home, admiring the dusted portraits, the well-stocked larder and the shining, open windows.

"You look all lighted up. Why, you're actually shining!" exclaimed Sara, as they stood in the former ballroom, where Sara was arranging a bowl of late roses freshly picked from the garden. Sylvia had just escorted the minister's wife, who had brought over a dish of jelly, into the kitchen. Aunts Hetty and Janet were laughing in the hall over some Sewing Circle gossip, while in the back parlor Olivia had found some dusty sheet music and was playing it on the antiquated piano.

The old lady looked out into the garden, where Andrew and Uncle Alec were diligently weeding. The honey-tinted sunshine fell thickly on the freshly mowed grass, the warm, pleasing smell of which drifted into the gracious room. "I feel so perfectly happy," she said with a long, rapturous sigh.

Just then Felix came running in, clutching

something behind his back. "C'mere, Sara. There's something I want to show you," he called, a suppressed grin glinting in his eyes.

Sara picked up a yellow rose and placed it in the glass bowl, studying the effect. She did not turn around. "Whatever it is, I don't care to see it," she answered, raising her nose in the air in just the way Felix found maddening.

He stared at her, his face turning a bright red. "Oh, go stick your head in pig swill!" he muttered, storming out of the room, "Now I'm never gonna show it to you."

For a moment after he left, Miss Lloyd continued to stare contentedly out the window. But when she looked over at Sara, her voice was stern. "What on earth can you be thinking of, child? Have you transferred the Lloyd curse onto your own head now?"

Sara looked up into a pair of angry eyes. There was no need for Miss Lloyd to say more. Sara knew exactly what she meant. She hesitated briefly, as though struggling with something inside herself. Then she laid down the bud she had been holding and raced outside after her cousin.

She found him out behind the old Lloyd stables, raking the grass with an air of glum discouragement.

"It's really kind of you to help clean up the estate, Felix," she began tentatively.

"Yeah, well, I don't have much choice. Mother and Aunt Hetty insisted. Father too."

"Well," Sara's voice feigned brightness. "I'm sure Miss Lloyd appreciates your work."

Felix did not respond.

This time Sara forced herself to say what she felt. "I haven't been very nice to you lately, Felix," she began, working her way up to an apology. But Felix got there first.

He turned quickly, his whole face breaking into a smile. "I'm sorry I said all those awful things to you, Sara, really I am. Soon as I said 'em, I knew I didn't mean any of 'em."

He pulled a square object from his back pocket and held it out to her. "I found this in the attic. I thought you should have it."

"What is it?"

A silver frame glinted in the sun. Even before she touched it, Sara knew it was something important.

"It's a picture of your mother, when she was your age."

Sara stared down at the faded photograph in astonishment. Her own face stared back at her. Her own hair, her own eyes—her own dear mother. She clutched the frame, as though she had been drowning and Felix had thrown her a rope.

First the piano, now this—both were evidence of her mother's former existence on the Island. They brought her closer, helped Sara feel less alone. Grateful tears started to her eyes. "Thank you, Felix. I've never seen a picture of her as a girl before."

Felix had given her back part of herself. All she had given him was anger, coldness, pride. She touched his arm. "Can you ever forgive me?"

Felix smiled his old, carefree smile. He had certainly been aptly named, she thought. "Gosh," he said. "I thought I was the one that had to be forgiven. But sure, I'll forgive you, if it makes you happy."

Sara threw her arms around him and hugged him. "*You've* made me happy, Felix," she said, "happy to have you for a cousin and a friend."

The welcome-home evening drew to a close with much laughter and merrymaking. Andrew Cameron insisted on driving everyone home, everyone, that is, except Sylvia, who had offered to stay with Miss Lloyd, in case she should need anything. Already a strong bond had sprung up between the old lady and the lighthearted young woman, who had taken to referring to Miss Lloyd as her "fairy godmother."

At first the old lady had laughingly objected. "Fairy godmothers—at least, in all the fairy tales I ever read—are somewhat apt to be queer, crotchety people, much more agreeable when wrapped up in mystery than when met face to face."

"Not at all. I'm convinced that mine is the very opposite, and that the better I become acquainted with her, the more charming I shall find her," answered Sylvia gaily.

According to the terms of the scholarship which Mr. Cameron had bestowed on Sylvia, she would not leave for Europe until the spring of the following year. This arrangement suited Sylvia perfectly. Having found in Miss Lloyd the family she had missed for so long, it would have broken her heart to have to part with her any sooner. Her only dilemma had consisted in where to stay. Despite Olivia's reassurances, she did not wish to outstay her welcome with Hetty at Rose Cottage.

And so, while Miss Lloyd was recuperating in Charlottetown, Sylvia had made inquiries of a widow who lived near the old Lloyd place and rented out rooms. The widow agreed to give her lodgings. But even the meager sum mentioned as payment would have meant a serious drain on Sylvia's limited resources.

The morning after her official homecoming, however, Miss Lloyd put Sylvia's problem to rest by formally inviting her to stay in the Lloyd mansion until she left for Europe. "And forever afterwards too," she added, a smile glimmering deep in her eyes. "From now on this will be your home, my dear, the place to which you belong, the place to which you always come back."

Sylvia, moved to tears at the thought of having a home once more, took the old lady's hand. She was filled with the glad knowledge that in accepting Margaret Lloyd's generosity, she was making both of them happy.

Epilogue

Margaret Lloyd lived up to the promise she had made to Sara on her sickbed. From that day forward she lived a very different sort of life. Instead of shutting herself off from the world as she had done for so many years, she now embraced it with open arms.

"I *can* help others," she told Sara one spring afternoon over tea, shortly before Sylvia's departure. "I've learned that money isn't the only power for helping people. Anyone who has sympathy and understanding to give, has a treasure that is without price."

She patted Sara's hand. "Sometimes it's the

young who teach the old, my dear. You taught me a valuable lesson about giving, Sara-girl, and I shall always be grateful to you for that."

Sara walked down the dusky driveway that evening in a mood of quiet contentment. She remembered the first time she had passed Miss Lloyd's gates, and how she had felt as though a hand had tugged at her heart.

It was strange, she thought, how people try to protect themselves and in doing so, sometimes hurt themselves more. It was strange how the *idea* of a curse could take shape in someone's mind. Miss Lloyd had allowed that idea to grow, until it spread like a weed, threatening to destroy her whole life, tangling it up in loneliness. Pride and fear had fed her idea, until it grew so strong that other people had begun to believe in it too. Love had rooted it out, though, and let the sun in.

Sara passed through the huge gates at the end of the driveway. They stood permanently open now, as if giving notice to the world of Miss Lloyd's change of heart. Already in Sara's head a story was taking shape, for creating and telling stories was what she liked to do best. This story concerned an old, old lady who lived all by herself in a strange, dark house. It began with a curse and ended with a blessing.... A smile played about Sara's lips as she strolled homewards.

Peg Bowen shifted a spruce branch and gazed through its dancing needles after the departing Sara. That young slip of a girl had turned out to be as fine a remedy as any she could hope to find growing in the earth. Ay, finer.

Well-satisfied, Peg lifted the glistening fish she had just caught, and headed up the driveway towards the lighted house. Old Lady Lloyd and her singing girl would feast on fresh fish this evening. And later, Peg would stand outside in the dark beneath the window and listen, puffing on her pipe, as the strains of *Greensleeves* and *My Love is Like a Red, Red Rose* floated out into the velvety spring night.

Bantam takes you on the...

Road to Avonlea *

Based on the Sullivan Films production adapted from the novels of
LUCY MAUD MONTGOMERY

☐ **THE JOURNEY BEGINS,** Book #1 $3.99/NCR
Dennis Adair and Janet Rosenstock   48027-8

☐ **THE STORY GIRL EARNS HER NAME,** $3.99/NCR
Book #2, Gail Hamilton   48028-6

☐ **SONG OF THE NIGHT,** Book #3 $3.99/NCR
Fiona McHugh   48029-4

☐ **THE MATERIALIZING OF DUNCAN** $3.99/NCR
MCTAVISH, Book #4, Heather Conkie   48030-8

☐ **QUARANTINE AT ALEXANDER** $3.99/NCR
ABRAHAM'S, Book #5, Fiona McHugh   48031-6

☐ **CONVERSIONS,** Book #6 $3.99/NCR
Gail Hamilton   48032-4

*ROAD TO AVONLEA is the trademark of Sullivan Films Inc.

Bantam Books, Dept SK50, 2451 South Wolf Road,
Des Plaines, IL 60018

Please send me the items I have checked above. I am enclosing
$_____ (please add $2.50 to cover postage and handling). Send
check or money order, no cash or C.O.D's please.

Mr/Mrs _____

Address _____

City/State _____ Zip _____

Please allow four to six weeks for delivery.   SK50-10/92
Prices and availability subject to change without notice.